# NEW HOKKAIDO

# NEW HOKKAIDO

JAMES McNAUGHTON

VICTORIA UNIVERSITY PRESS

VICTORIA UNIVERSITY PRESS
Victoria University of Wellington
PO Box 600 Wellington
vup.victoria.ac.nz

National Library of New Zealand Cataloguing-in-Publication Data

McNaughton, James.
New Hokkaido / James McNaughton.
ISBN 978-0-86473-976-6
I. Title.
NZ823.3—dc 23

Published with the assistance of a grant from

Printed by Printlink, Wellington

for Elizabeth

## Acknowledgements

Thanks to the New Zealand Society of Authors, Sam McNaughton, Geoff Walker, the late Michael Gifkins, Garth Dawson, Rodney Smith, Fergus Barrowman, Ashleigh Young and the team at VUP.

Above all, thanks to Elizabeth, my wife and first reader, for her love and belief.

# Contents

# Prologue

On the night of 6 December 1941, with the Japanese fleet poised 400 km north of Hawaii in preparation for an attack on the US naval base at Pearl Harbour, Emperor Hirohito had a vision of an incinerated Japanese city. Believing it to be a divine warning, he called back the carriers. The United States did not play a combat role in World War II. Japan bypassed Australia and invaded New Zealand in 1942. When the USSR defeated Nazi Germany and liberated France in 1946, it became the new ruler of Europe. A stand-off between the USSR and Great Britain (propped up by the United States) began. Japan, under threat of attack from the United States, formed the Red Sun Alliance with the USSR in 1946 and both countries quickly completed the conquest of China in a two-front attack. By 1987, trade between the Red Sun Alliance and the United States has resumed.

# Chapter 1:

# The English Academy

Ten Japanese adults, seated in two rows of five in the little classroom, are bent over their books writing their hobbies and the hobbies they guess their partner in the other row has. Chris Ipswitch stands before the blackboard, six foot three, broad-shouldered, the tallest in the room and at twenty the youngest. He wears a black suit and a white shirt, and has buzz-cut black hair and a cheerful expression on his handsome white face. He wants the class to end on a high note, to send his students out on a cloud so he can drift out too, out of the staffroom early and into the evening, into the secret New Zealand Culture Meeting at a house in Mount Victoria. He's worked nights and weekends for three months straight now and it's a Friday night and he wants to have a drink and meet some women. The thought of the Culture Meeting, his first, stokes his cheerful expression.

But it all depends on the deputy principal letting him go early. The excuse he has prepared is that he would like to play evening touch rugby just this once because the team's short. It's a request he hopes will elicit some sympathy now that he has to work weekends and is unable to play on

Saturdays. Although Chris had known rugby was important to him when he gave it up for work, he didn't realise just how important. He has lost much more than just the eighty minutes on Saturday.

Yet he's grateful for his job. He's the only Kiwi employed in a teaching role at the Academy, and his pay reflects that honour. His friends, by comparison, have casual labouring jobs with low pay, long hours and no security. Chris hears a lot about it. Those who have proved reliable on the last job are first on the list. But if a man misses a day, be it through sickness or a workplace injury or whatever reason, he's bumped off the list and the first man waiting gets the job. Getting onto the list can take months of turning up at worksites pre-dawn with dozens of other hungry men and hoping someone screws up.

He has learned the names and faces of this new class. He has learned their hair as they keep their heads diligently down and compose full, natural-sounding sentences. Three students have dark black hair, one glossy black, three normal black, two a hint of very dark brown; one is flecked with grey. Another of the glossy black heads has a streak of blue dye in it. Their hair is spiky, wavy, straight, lank, luxurious, prim; all different, no repeat categories. His eye returns to the blue streak. It's unusual for Japanese to dye their hair. He knows she's a Settler because he has sneaked a look at the file: a civilian sent to the furthest colony of the Empire rather than prison in Japan. Two of the men are also Settlers. What their crimes were he doesn't know. He's looked for missing fingertips, the mark of dishonour meted out by the Yakuza, but he hasn't had a clear view yet. There may be prosthetics involved. In any case, he has twelve weeks of this course to get a good look at their fingertips. The three of them sit separately and he wonders if they know one another.

The woman with blue hair looks up. Chris will make eye

contact if she raises her hand. She doesn't. After a long time she looks down.

'Okay, who's first?' he says. 'Is there a volunteer? Anyone?'

Some rueful looks. They're enjoying it.

'Okay,' he says to the girl with the blue hair, 'at the back, Miss Kurosawa. Please tell us your hobbies and then guess your partner's hobbies.'

She looks at him as she tells the class: 'I like to watch TV and sleep.'

'Oh,' says the class. 'Yes.'

Miss Kurosawa turns to a woman in the row beside her, a general's middle-aged wife. 'I guess . . . am guessing?' She looks at Chris again.

'Either,' he says, with a happy smile. '"I guess", or, "I'm guessing that you". . .'

'I'm guessing that you like to play basketball and listen to music.'

The class titters at the thought of the venerable general's wife playing basketball. He knows she meant him, and it's a pretty good guess. He is a lock, a jumping line-out specialist, or was. Music he loves, especially the banned work of Johnny Lennon. Her accurate guess, the guess of a criminal, makes him uncomfortable. The general's wife says her hobbies. Laughter comes with each disclosure and guess. The exercise is going as he had hoped. Please, let me go early, he thinks, and imagines the deputy principal waving him away. Yet part of him hopes there will be no wave, just an annoyed grunt of refusal, because the meeting is very dangerous. And yet the danger is exciting. He laughs automatically, following the class's cue, delighted, thinking of hot sake and girls and New Zealand music in a secret basement.

He stands by the door maintaining a respectful bow as the class file out. Even bowing, he's taller than they are.

Maybe that's why I can do this, he thinks. Some nod slightly in return. Miss Kurosawa is last, fiddling with her bag. The room is empty when she stands in front of him, tall, taller than most Japanese men, and skinny. Her eyes have a sleepy, sardonic quality. She's older than him, maybe twenty-five. Her lips are full and expressive. She pouts and then speaks.

'Can you give me a private lesson?'

'No. I'm sorry, Miss Kurosawa. That's illegal.' He is not even remotely interested. He would lose his job and to make matters worse she's a Settler. She's just trouble.

'Oh. What a shame.' She speaks English well, but he doesn't ask where she learned it.

'Thank you for your enquiry,' he says.

She turns her lips down in a sad clown's expression and is gone, leaving a wake of musky perfume. Trouble.

He packs up quickly, excited, sure for some reason that the deputy principal will let him go early. As he closes the classroom door his older colleague, Masuda, simultaneously closes his.

'Sorry, sir,' Chris says, as he must to Masuda for occupying the same space unexpectedly. Masuda glares at him. Deep furrows line his forehead. His spectacles flash. He is always angry with Chris because he, Masuda, is an English teacher who can't really speak English, and although he's forty-five and Chris is only twenty, Chris is a much better teacher. The fact that Chris is a native speaker doesn't diminish the insult to Masuda's pride, and Chris must always use the most respectful Japanese speech when addressing him and suffer sharp rebukes for the slightest slip. Masuda's spectacles flash again. He's building up a full head of steam. Probably, Chris thinks, because my class could be heard laughing and left the room happier than his. He stands rigidly, waiting for his senior to leave first. But of course Masuda doesn't leave; he marches toward Chris, who reminds himself that the man's bark is worse than his bite.

'Teach your subject. Don't play games.'

Chris bows. 'Yes, sir.'

Masuda turns and Chris remains bowing until the strike of his heels has echoed away.

Chris enters the staffroom with his eyes down, making himself a shadow. His desk, cluttered like the others with piles of books and documents on the verge of toppling, is at the back of the room beside the rear entrance. Unusually, the teachers have gathered at the front, before the platform on which the principal and deputy principal sit. The senior Business English teacher stands in the centre of the group, holding court. Excited, he strikes his palm with his fist repeatedly.

'Yes,' he cries, 'it sets a precedent. If the uprising in Paris is not put down, France will fall. Already there are stirrings in Berlin. Even the *Germans* are talking about freedom. The Soviet Union must fix its internal problems or it will cease to exist and we will be left alone to hold China. Will the US stand and watch us in the Pacific then? No!'

The teacher's cry of anger sends a shiver up Chris's spine. He tidies his desk quietly, invisibly. There is silence. They've seen me, he thinks. He closes a drawer and stands, as if deep in thought but hurrying, oblivious to everything but his own desk. Picking up his briefcase, he turns to notice the silent knot of teachers. Expressing surprise, he bows and apologises.

The teachers reluctantly disband and return to their desks.

He remains bowing until all are seated, then he approaches the altar-like structure at the front of the room. 'Sorry,' he says as he bows to the deputy principal.

A grunt. The frog-like hand waves as soon as he begins his request. Chris is dismissed.

They can talk now, he thinks as he walks quickly away

down the corridor, fighting an urge to punch the air and run out into the street. The news he has heard is even more thrilling because it will be gold at the New Zealand Culture Meeting and sure to impress the women there. And I have a job, he thinks. Not many my age have money. If I meet someone I'll be able to take her out.

He steps into the early darkness of June and pauses at the top of the school steps, between the armed sentries on either side of the door. A gust of wind buffets him and whips the large Japanese flag high above the huge concrete Central Administration Centre that dominates uptown. But higher than the red circle on white, great clouds are tumbling across the dark blue sky in the west, rolling and roiling as they go, as if freed and stampeding all the way from Paris.

# Chapter 2:

# A New Zealand Culture Meeting

The first heavy drops of rain strike as Chris finds the letterbox numbered 87. He's fifteen minutes late and puffing, having run up the hill from the tram stop at the end of Courtenay Place, carrying a six-pack of Asahi Super Dry and eating four takoyaki balls. The takoyaki wasn't good, more pickled ginger and green onion than octopus, but he didn't have time to go to his usual shop. Still, his hunger has been quelled and he managed to keep the sauce off his suit.

The letters he makes out in the gloom are hand-painted on wooden postboxes; maybe it's 81 rather than 87. No, he finds 85 in a nearby pool of darkness under a tree. The street is rank and overgrown, and smells like the bush. The Japanese don't like to live on hills. Their preferred flat areas are well maintained, well lit, and well signposted. It's 87 then, definitely, same as the year. His mouth is dry, and not just from the run up the hill. The possibility of a patrol bursting into the meeting has become very real. He imagines the horror of being lined up and screamed at, punched and kicked repeatedly as summary executions proceed one by one, by bullet and sword, until, humiliated and terrified, he

17

is executed. He checks the number on the rotting wooden box one last time.

The house, with one room dimly lit, is at the bottom of a long flight of subsiding concrete steps overgrown with fennel. It's dark under the trees and he relies on the faded white paint marking the edge of each step to guide him down. The glowing light looks warm through heavy curtains and he's excited at the prospect of who will be there. He's also comforted by the house's distance from the road and the surrounding trees and thick undergrowth, which will help conceal his escape if the worst happens. The iron roof bangs and pops under intensifying rain as he descends.

At the porch he is dismayed to see no shoes. I'm at the wrong house, he thinks, or else the meeting's been cancelled. Now the meeting is off, his fear has gone and he is unequivocally disappointed, angry even. A girlish giggle in the dark above thrills him. Two figures have begun to descend. Both women. Filled with hope, he knocks gently on the door.

'Gidday, mate.' A red-faced man of about thirty, more than a little drunk and excited, seizes his hand and pumps it. Under his unbuttoned flannel shirt is a T-shirt depicting a sushi roll under a crossed red circle, like a No Smoking sign. It's a brave display: opening the door to a Japanese patrol wearing that T-shirt would result in a crippling beating, if he was lucky. His hair is teased at the front and streaked with red dye. He wears shorts and gumboots. 'A suit?' he asks. His brow furrows and his eyes roll anxiously over Chris's shoulder up to the dark road.

'I came straight from work,' Chris says.

'Right, you must be . . .'

'Chris Ipswitch.'

'That's right. Good on ya, mate. Come in, come in.'

When Chris bends to unzip his vinyl shoes, the man

cries, 'No, mate, leave them on. No Jap rules here. Come in, come in.'

'Cheers. There are a couple more just behind me.'

The man's bleary looping eyes take a while to find their target. 'Mind your step, ladies,' he calls over Chris's shoulder.

After cramming his beer in the fridge, Chris enters the dim lounge. Already more than a dozen are there. The legal limit for a house is eight. Three are women, and the two behind him makes five. The young men wear thick woollen bush shirts, shorts, and gumboots. A trestle table covered with an old New Zealand flag, and bearing a pavlova, saveloys and sausage rolls, dominates the room. Chris takes a deep breath. The flag means they will be in serious trouble if a patrol raids them: the owner of the house will almost certainly be shot on the spot. Beyond that, the number of murders and the severity of the beatings will depend, to a large extent, on the patrol commander's mood. On a shitty night like this, things might go very badly.

The figures standing around the flag table in their bulky bush-shirt uniforms radiate a military strength, yet they are just young men his own age and unlikely to be armed with anything more than knives. The house feels vulnerable. Violence is in the air. He'd imagined a cellar or basement with proper security, not a wooden bungalow with a man at the door in a joke T-shirt, too drunk to keep proper watch. I can't just turn and leave, he thinks. Or can I? He's mulling over the consequences of leaving when he makes out the welcome face of Marty, the friend who secured his invitation. Marty, an open-side flanker who's often first to the breakdown, is at his side in a flash to shake hands. His curly blond hair, once his pride and joy—or his mother's, to be fair—is already falling out. This tragically vanishing fleece is a source of much piss-taking in the team. He's a popular guy.

'You made it,' Marty says with a grin, eyeing Chris's suit. 'Come straight from work, bro?'

'Yeah, they had a secret meeting and let me go. I was lucky.' Chris takes out his packet of Japanese Silk Cut cigarettes manufactured for the Western market and offers one; he's happy to note his hand is steady. Hearing the door wrenched open, he flinches. No, it's another guest; the so-called guard brays happily in greeting and closes it again.

'I have an ashtray,' Marty says, lighting up. He's holding a full beer bottle and an empty bottle for ash, and smoking at the same time.

Chris grins at his juggling routine. 'Good to see you, bro. Good to get out. Jesus.'

'Yeah man, it's like you've been under arrest. Should be a good night, eh? Seen anything you like the look of yet?'

A belligerent voice. 'Too formal, mate. Japs dress up for parties. Kiwis go casual.'

Chris guesses the man who has planted himself next to him, clad in a bush shirt, jeans and gumboots, is a prop. Yet even he has flouncy hair browned with dye. He sticks his hand out and they shake as Marty makes introductions. His name is Stew and he's just moved down from Taranaki to play rugby. Marty explains that Chris can't play this year because of his job. Stew says he's heard about him, the missing lock, and it's a damn shame.

The two girls who came in behind Chris enter the lounge, glowing and bright-eyed from their walk in the night air, surprisingly tall in their high heels, which he likes, but their long loose dresses and old cardigans look odd. He can see they've powdered their noses since arriving, but their big hair has been somewhat naturalised by the weather, a good thing in his opinion. They smile and join the group, shake hands and exchange names. He likes the look of Emily, a busty brunette with brown skin and a bright smile. Neither she nor her friend has the affected inward-pointing toes and helium voices of J-Pop idols that an increasing number of young Kiwi women are adopting.

The prop taps the ash from his cigarette into Marty's bottle. 'Good man,' he tells him.

The girls smile and Chris offers his packet of expensive Silk Cut. They both accept and soon they're tapping ash into the bottle Marty gallantly wields.

'Your dress is a little formal,' Emily notes, with a twinkle in her eye.

He wants to tell her he has money, prospects, a life. 'I came straight from work.'

'What do you do?' She's interested; they all are, even the thick-necked prop, Stew.

'English teacher.'

'Where?'

He translates the Japanese name: 'The Language Academy.' Met with blank looks, he adds, 'It's north of the intersection of Teramachi and Oshikoji Streets.'

'He means on Willis Street,' says Stew, and Chris is embarrassed to have used the official Japanese address system. 'Jeez, I know that,' Stew continues, pressing home his advantage in front of the women, 'and I'm from Taranaki.'

Thankfully, the women don't laugh.

'How'd you get that job, mate?' asks Stew. The question is aggressive, as if Chris has done something unsavoury to get it, something unpatriotic.

'I got a high score on the test.'

'What test, mate?'

'An open test at the Academy. A public test. Anyone could walk in and take it.'

'I didn't hear about that,' says Emily. 'I've been looking for work for ages.'

He feels he must be completely honest with her,

21

particularly at this early stage in their relationship. 'Well, it was a Japanese test. You have to be good at Japanese to teach English. That's the main requirement.'

'That's fucked up, mate. Why are you so good at Jap?'

Ignoring the prop, Chris lights another cigarette. Obviously, he thinks, because I'm good at it. He knows Emily will understand.

'Why are you so good at Jap?' repeats the prop.

'It's compulsory. I picked it up.'

The prop waves his hand before his face. 'Shit, mate, how do you smoke those things?'

Silk Cut are only 75% tobacco. 'For good health,' he replies.

'It's like smoking lawn clippings,' says Stew, wrinkling his nose.

'I wouldn't know,' Chris says, without smiling. 'I'm not from Taranaki.'

Stew doesn't smile either. He drops his butt in Marty's bottle, produces a packet of Hillary, lights up, and blows smoke in Chris's direction.

The girls have spotted someone across the room they know and wave with their fingers in greeting. Obviously relieved to escape the growing unpleasantness between Chris and Stew, they go to see their friend. It seems to Chris that the sun has gone behind a cloud. And the prop is still in his face.

'You don't just *pick up* Japanese like a suitcase, mate. You have to work at it.'

Chris decides he likes Stew's forthrightness. Honesty is a valuable trait. He's right, his line of questioning is actually reasonable, and he will tell Stew the truth: that he is the famous Patrick Ipswitch's younger brother and was exposed to a different environment from most kids. It's a good story, he knows, and he's about to launch into it when a wiry elderly man standing at the head of the flagged trestle table calls for quiet.

Conversation stops and the knots of people in conversation open up and turn to the speaker. Maybe twenty people, a thrilling number in a private house, now encircle the table. The steely little man is neatly dressed in a polo shirt, pleated trousers and hard shoes. His hair, although entirely grey, is thick and swept to the side.

'My name's Brian Murray,' he says in a strong, clear voice. 'John invited me here as a kind of "cultural consultant", I think he called it. He's been kind enough to host this event and I think we should thank him for it.'

The host, a gingery man of thirty-five in a vintage corduroy jacket, woollen suit trousers and black dress shoes like Brian's, raises a hand and smiles to a ripple of applause.

'Let me tell you a little bit about myself,' continues Brian. 'I was an artillery gunner in the war. I fought in Burma and was lucky to get out. Back in New Zealand I manned the guns at Makara and am proud to have helped sink the heavy cruiser *Maya*.' Everyone applauds, someone whistles. Brian's face falls. 'I had fifteen years hard labour in Featherston after that and saw most of my friends die. Mainly from illness and starvation, but some were beheaded.'

As Brian speaks of the atrocities in the camps, the younger people glance around the room at one another. Chris is the tallest and the only male not dressed as a farmer. Judging by Brian's smart attire, it appears to him that the Kiwi dress around him is not authentic. Everyone looks like low-paid labourers, which is exactly what they are now under Japanese rule. Why not dress as managers, as people who own their own land and control their own destiny? And surely, he thinks, we used to leave our gumboots outside rather than traipse sheep shit through the house. Emily's outfit, with its ancient heavy cardigan, is disappointing. Her big bust and long neck would look spectacular in a little black dress. She should wear jewellery, put her hair up. The effect would be stunning. She flicks her eyes at him and he smiles warmly, confident of his feelings for her. After a very brief shy smile in return, she concentrates on Brian, who is rounding up his POW experiences.

'I know you've all heard stories like this before,' he says sadly, 'and I don't want to spoil the party. It should be a celebration. A celebration of who we are, not what those bastards tell us we are.' The applause is strong. 'John, your kind and courageous host, asked me to duplicate a genuine Kiwi party. Well, this is what we used to do forty-odd years ago when we were free. Before we became tenants in our own country. The food's out, as you can see, and there's not a single bloody raw fish in sight. Thank you, ladies, for bringing a plate. Of course in our day you wouldn't have to drop it around in secret a day or two beforehand, so extra credit must go where extra credit's due. Let's hear it for the ladies.' Chris contributes energetically to the round of applause, which the women instinctively acknowledge with a bow.

'No bowing!' The gleeful cry is of someone catching out a mate in a drinking game. Heads turn to the red-faced man who has been on door duty.

'Good Kiwi food,' says Brian, and everyone turns back to him. 'It's all cooked!' He pauses for more applause, which comes less certainly. 'I don't know about this sitting on the floor business they make us do we when we go out. It seems another way of keeping us down.' He senses he's losing the room. 'What was natural to us was that the men would relax in the kitchen standing up and the women in the lounge, sitting down with a cup of tea.' Sensing disapproval, he adds, 'Or some vodka and lemonade. Then, after a couple of drinks and a nibble we'd have a little dance to the gramophone.

Please enjoy yourselves. You'll make your ancestors proud.'

Brian is applauded warmly, but his remark about separating the sexes into kitchen and lounge is not what Chris wanted to hear. He tries to catch Emily's eye on the way to the kitchen but she's busy talking to her friend. Someone behind him says, 'Nice suit, mate,' as the men crowd into the kitchen, gumboots clomping.

'Better access to the piss, lads,' says a tall, thin, pale-faced boyish man with a yellow-and-brown mullet. 'Our ancestors knew what they were doing.' His bush shirt is too big, like a dress on him, and his thin white legs disappear into oversize gumboots with a hole in the toe. Yet his voice is surprisingly deep.

While Chris is getting a beer from the fridge, someone else says, 'Nice suit.' He turns to see the hard faces of twelve men in a circle, bulky in their woollen bush shirts. The comment could have come from any of them.

The circle parts for Brian, who raises his bottle. 'More men in the kitchen than allowed in a house.'

'Hear, hear.'

'Sweet.'

They all touch bottles, a circle of men reaching into the centre. It's unusual, different from the strictly monitored rugby team meetings in the clubhouse, and electrifying, a situation full of possibilities both exciting and terrifying. Despite his nervousness, Chris nods his gratitude to Marty for inviting him. He wants to share the news about Paris he heard in the staffroom but knows he must wait for Brian to speak again. The older man looks thoughtful and tired at close range, a lucky survivor, as if speaking about the death camp has released distressing memories and drained him. But he has made it, somehow, and has wisdom to share. He appears to stare at something in another dimension, something vivid but hard to make sense of. The silence becomes awkward and Chris is about to speak when Brian's eyes focus and come to life. He blinks slowly and nods his head.

'Auckland tomorrow. Should be a good game.'

'We'll need to close Kirwan down.'

'Yep.'

'He won't get the ball, mate. We'll starve them of possession.'

Chris is deeply disappointed. As the conversation stutters around him, lurching from injuries to the weather report to Gallagher's form with the boot, he wonders if their conversation would be more fluid and abstract in Japanese. Maybe our English is rustier than we realise, he thinks.

When the conversation falters, Brian says, 'I'd better check on the ladies.'

'When do we get to check on them?' asks Chris, when he's safely out of earshot.

'After we've sunk some more piss,' says the prop.

'Reckon,' says another man. 'I'll need a few before the dance.'

'I've never done that kind of thing before.'

'Dancing?'

'Yeah.'

'I did once, but not in gumboots.'

'Ha ha ha.'

'I went to take mine off at the door and got yelled at.'

'Same, bro.'

'So, this dancing thing—'

'The only fuckin' thing the Japs taught me was to bow and shuffle.'

'Yellow fucking scum.'

After a round of abuse, to which Chris does not contribute, there comes a silence. The dance still looms.

'J-Popsters do Western dancing now.'

'Don't watch that shit.'

'Fuck, mate.'

'I saw it on a screen downtown. I couldn't help seeing it.'

'Just bounce on the spot,' Marty says, 'and look happy.'

'I could murder one of those sausage rolls.'

'Me too, bro.'

'I think the ladies go first.'

'They'll eat the fucking lot if we're not careful.'

A man leaves the circle and peers into the lounge. 'It's all right, mate,' he reports upon his return, 'hardly touching them. Don't like your chances of getting any pavlova, though.'

'That'd be right.'

A general laugh ensues and Chris sees the hard faces around him relax properly for the first time. Yet he has the feeling no one is quite sure why they're laughing.

'Round two,' announces the tall thin man in his oddly deep voice as he opens the fridge. 'To a free New Zealand,' is the toast, and the bottoms of the bottles go up. Glug, glug, glug. As the third round is taken from the fridge and distributed, the man says to Chris, 'What's with the suit?'

Clearly everyone wants to know. Chris tells them he came straight from work and answers the same line of questioning the prop asked. Suspicious eyes are on him. Their faces are reddening from heat, from wearing bush shirts indoors, and from beer. Wanting to puncture their disapproval, he tells them what he heard in the staffroom, but changes the speaker from a teacher to the principal for heightened effect. It doesn't help. They don't care about Paris. They don't trust him and have the right to beat him up. In fact, they're obliged to. He looks to Marty, his friend.

'Nervous Japs in the staffroom?' says Marty. 'Must be bad. Must be terrible, in fact. Excellent news.'

No one says anything. They look at Chris as if he's a spy.

He realises that he was right about the aura of violence he sensed upon arrival, but he'd never imagined it would take the form of a beating at the hands of his countrymen.

'Paris is a long way from here, mate,' Stew tells him. 'Te Urewera is what you should be thinking about.'

'True, mate. True.'

He means the Maori guerrillas in the mountainous bush in the east of the North Island, the only territory in New Zealand not controlled by the Empire. Though possibly not for much longer, Chris thinks. The Imperial Japanese Army has launched a major offensive with helicopters, rockets and thermal-imaging devices fresh from Russia. The guerrillas have small arms and homemade bombs, and starvation and disease.

'They're just fighting for survival,' he says.

'Fuck you, man.' It's the boy with the deep voice.

Someone steps back and pulls his bush shirt off over his head. Standing in a black singlet, flexing mighty biceps, he stares at Chris. A couple more follow his lead. They're dressed the same. The black singlets are a declaration of war; they are ready to fight.

'We need outside help,' Chris says mildly, although his heart gallops and breath comes quickly. 'Looks like we're getting some in Europe.'

'We need both, man,' says the deep-voiced boy, whose bone-thin legs indicate why he's left his bush shirt on. 'Inside and outside. What's your name anyway?'

'Chris Ipswitch.'

Using Japanese pronunciation, the boy says, 'Ip-u-sa-wit-ich-u?'

'My bro.'

'The sumo champ?'

'Yep.'

'Get the fuck out of here!'

'Into the lounge?' With the ladies, he means: a failed attempt at humour.

Several voices are raised at once, and a surge of grudging respect comes his way. They look at him again, recalibrating his suit and fancy job. But the deep voice wins out. 'Your bro shacked up with a Jap and had her bastard baby.'

'Sarah's my niece. She's a great kid.'

Brian's back with the host, the gingery man in vintage corduroy who has been with the ladies all along. It's a privilege Chris is willing to concede, given the risk he's taking. 'Whoa, whoa,' says the host, flapping his arms, 'keep it down, boys. We have to watch the noise.'

'Yeah, but Mr Suit here is Ip-u-sa-wit-ich-u's little brother.'

Brian looks pained. 'Look, let's all be friends. Come and have a sausage roll.'

'He works at the Language Academy, too,' offers the prop. 'Bet he's a green.'

It's true; Chris does have a green ID card, indicating his high level of trustworthiness. It came with his job and he wonders what to say.

'He's cool,' says Marty, sparing him the need to reply. 'I invited him. I've known him for years. Damn fine lock.'

Brian processes this. 'Do you have contact with your brother?'

'Yeah. I love the guy.'

The boy with the deep voice and skinny white legs appeals to Brian. 'He shacked up with that Jap bitch and had a half-breed with her.'

Chris remains calm. 'That half-breed's my niece. My brother was an athlete. He was the best. Everyone loved him when he was beating the Japs. Remember? He was a national hero. Suddenly he's gone from hero to zero just because he fell in love with a woman. She doesn't care about the Empire. She just wants to raise a family.'

Red-faced from beer and his bush shirt, a young man who hasn't spoken before says with great intensity: 'He's disgraced our glorious dead.'

'Shame.'

'True.'

Chris's heart sinks. The kitchen is against him. The black singlets are ready to pounce. It seems the only thing preventing them from beating him up is the noise it will make.

'C'mon,' says Marty, 'Chris is solid.' His opinion carries enough weight to defer violence for a moment.

'I love my bro,' says Chris. 'I'll leave.'

'No, don't do that,' says Brian. 'We're not sending you out like this.'

Chris becomes aware of rain lashing the roof and kitchen window.

'You fellows join the ladies in the lounge. Now, don't just stand around the food table and talk about rugby. Pick one item and take it with you when you make conversation with a lady. It's up to you to ask them to dance—don't let them down. I'll have a word to Chris here in private.'

No one moves a muscle so Brian leads him away, moving quickly and fluidly down the hall. He turns into a bedroom and Chris pauses, fearing a trap. Yet he follows anyway, into the musty dark, where he expects the steely little man will try to kill him. Brian snaps on a light and closes the door.

'You work at the Language Academy in Willis Street?'

'Yes. I came straight from there.'

'Look, can you help us?'

'Us?'

'Free New Zealand.'

'How?'

'Give us the names of Settlers, if you can. They don't love

30

the Empire. They can be useful to us.'

'I can give you two names now.'

'Good man.'

He gives the names of the two new men, but not the girl with blue hair. Brian looks at him, weighs him up with the skill of a veteran, a man who survived fifteen years in the death camp in Featherston. Chris thinks, what did you have to do to survive?

'Why did you come here?' Brian asks him. His eyes are pale blue and unblinking.

'I, um . . . I wanted to meet some women.'

After a long, searching moment, Brian holds out his hand. 'I trust you.' They shake. 'I want you to stay. We'll have some music and all leave here as friends.'

Not likely, Chris thinks. They'll jump me on the road.

Just as he enters the lounge, his back tingling as Brian follows close behind him, the song on the stereo ends. The trestle table has gone and everyone is spread out, standing uncertainly as the host takes a single off the turntable. There are more men than women. Chris knows, by the awkwardness, the stony faces and averted eyes, that he's been talked about. The men have told the women he's no good, not to be trusted. Rain drums on the roof. Emily won't look at him. Marty, his friend, comes from his little group and offers a cigarette. Other people light up. He wishes the music would start but the host is scrupulously careful with his records, carefully de-sleeving an LP, removing it from its inner plastic sheath, then holding the vinyl disc by the edges with his palms. Finally an electric crackle, a thickening of silence, and the familiar, beloved burst of feedback that heralds the classic opening track, 'Losing My Head', from *Lennon Live in Levin*. It's one of Chris's all-time favourites. As Johnny screams 'Banzaaaaaaaai!' the weight that has been bearing down on him shifts. The hair-raising voice and thunderous band bring the room to motion, albeit uncertain motion. The men are unsure whether to lift their feet, and they chug their arms like toy trains. There is some bouncing, the flap and wallop of gumboots, and grim smiling. They peep at each other for clues; abruptly change style. It's morbid. Torture. He feels eyes flick over him, the tallest man in the room, and thinks of his brother dancing, of his power and restraint, his surprising lightness. Watch me, Emily, he thinks, I'm enjoying myself rather than suffering. He is. He loves this fucking song, and the way Lennon's rhythm guitar nails the offbeat. As eyes flash over him he senses a shift in the room. They're following his basic up-and-down motion. You boys can learn something, he thinks. The prop drops his hand circles. Side-shuffling is abandoned. Someone in a black singlet steps out of his gumboots. But just as he feels the room start to jump, the host lifts the needle mid-track—*squip*. Sabotage, Chris thinks. He's sabotaged me.

The light comes on, and the owner, who has been unusually calm about the whole situation until now, is flushed and nervous. 'Sorry guys, it's late already. And we do have some other business to attend to. If the rugby players and Ed, Mark, Matt, Graeme, Grant and Peter, yes, I think that's everyone, could have a word with Brian in the back room, and the ladies leave now so there isn't a stampede out of here. I have a car for anyone who wants a ride.'

To his horror, Chris sees he's the only male not directed into the back room. Marty's face is cloudy as he disappears down the hall with the rest of the men, all of them, in their black singlets and flannel and bush shirts. The women won't look at him as they leave to put on their coats. The host is at the door with a torch, in the fancy corduroy jacket he's worn all night. It's still raining and all five women want a lift. 'Just give us ten minutes' head start, mate,' he tells Chris brusquely. 'Then you can be on your way.'

He turns away and looks out the window, pretending to assess the weather, hoping Emily will come into the lounge and say bye, or just pop her head around the door. The back door closes. She's gone. Listening keenly, he hears muted exclamations and laughter as the group negotiate the stairs in clipping high heels. A final laugh up on the road, a car door slams. Silence from the back room: plotting. He's alone.

Humiliated, he takes a beer from the fridge and sculls it. He opens another for the wet and cold road home. I should've stayed at work, he thinks bitterly. His anger, always deep-seated and slow to take, begins to burn. *I'll take that Lennon record.* But as he searches the spines, arranged in alphabetical order, he realises it will be missed and he will be the prime suspect. For that reason the remaining beer in the fridge is also off limits. He scans the kitchen and his eyes settle on the phone. A toll call is something he can take.

He dials the familiar number and waits while listening for a change in the house.

'Chris?'

'You know it, bro.' He lets out a breath. Already he feels better.

'I've been trying to ring you.' There's a sharp and unfamiliar note in Patrick's voice. 'I even rang the Academy.'

'Why? What's happened?'

'Sarah . . . I've got bad news, Chris, sorry. Sarah's been murdered.'

'What?'

'Someone broke her neck in Hagley Park.'

'Huh?' Sarah is three.

'It was instant. A professional hit.'

'Oh, no.' He believes it. Tears fill his eyes.

'Chiyo took her to the playground there. She was talking to a friend for two minutes, looked up, and Sarah was gone.

She found her under a hedge.'

'Who did it?'

'I don't know, man. A lot of people don't like me.' The sound of his brother weeping.

'I'm coming down Patrick. I'm coming down now.' He waits. 'I love you, man. Hang·in there.'

A groan is the reply. His brother, the sumo champion, the strongest and bravest man he knows, is unable to speak.

A flare of voices in the back room announces agreement or a vote passed. He knows that many of them will greet the news of Sarah's death with pleasure, even delight. He can't stand here holding the phone any longer. 'I'm sorry,' he whispers. 'I have to go.'

# Chapter 3:

# The Lyttelton Ferry

It's a clear, still night, and cold. The late sailing is running late. Chris's breath steams as he stands on the top deck in the long woollen overcoat Patrick gave him a couple of years ago. It's a hand-me-down, and too big, but beautifully cut and very warm. After reading an underground pamphlet on a tram that morning, in which Sarah's death was blamed on the Japanese, he plans to make most of the trip to Lyttelton above deck. In the pamphlet article, senior Japanese officials described Sarah as 'an affront to the Empire' and 'a mongrel to be put down'. Then on National Radio her death was described in Japanese as 'an act of domestic terrorism'. He doesn't want to go below and drink hot sake like everyone else in case he's recognised. There would be no end to the arguing and no escape. The second-class cabins with eight bunks are off-limit for the same reason. Black seawater begins to churn at the stern and the rail vibrates under his hand. A few passengers come up for a look, Japanese tourists mostly. One couple takes turns posing for photos under the limp New Hokkaido flag, a Tourism New Zealand initiative, in which the Union Jack in the corner of the banned New

Zealand flag has been replaced by the Rising Sun. Some Kiwis are glad to see the Southern Cross flying again in any form; others see it as a gross defacement. More cameras flash. Chris turns away. In whatever tourist hot spot the Southern Cross flies, the standard Japanese flags fly higher.

Chris pulls his collar higher. Inexplicably, he has forgotten his beanie. The boat shudders and there is a sense of hard-earned motion. Lights on the water shatter and re-gather in the swelling wake. Most of the houses on the hills are dark, either to save electricity or because they have none. Yet the sky above the railway station glows majestically. The bright raised mall that surrounds it, known as Little Japan, allows the occupiers to come in and shop and dine and dance, then leave by rail again without touching the ground. Chris has never been there. The dingy pachinko parlours, pool halls, bowling alleys and karaoke parlours he knows uptown will be closed by now. The restaurants and yakitori bars along Oriental Bay are closed or closing. A string of coloured lightbulbs wink out. He thinks of Sarah, how he'll be unable to stay for her funeral, and wonders if he should have left for Christchurch a bit later. But funerals are for the living, he reminds himself, and his brother needs him now rather than later. He's alone, staring at a yellow window in Seatoun, when a woman speaks to him in Japanese.

'Are you cold, Teacher?'

Miss Kurosawa, the Settler, stands hatless at the rail, six feet away, staring at Seatoun. Her hair, with its streak of dark blue, is tugged and worried by the wind. The New Hokkaido flag snaps overhead.

'Good evening, Miss Kurosawa.'

'Aren't you cold?' She takes out a woollen hat, pulls it on and stares at the lights. Then she glances at him and pushes out her lower lip as if to say, well, here we are.

It's not a normal interaction. He realises that his formal

politeness is not required. 'I forgot my hat,' he says.

'I recognised your hair. Why is it so short? Like a soldier's.'

'I cut it myself. To save money.'

'Mm.' Even in her coat she looks thin. 'I won't sleep tonight,' she says. He can tell she means it. It's the immediate problem he faces as well.

'Are you cold, Miss Kurosawa?'

'Yes.' She looks at him, then looks around the empty deck, and he expects her to go. 'Why are you going to Christchurch?' she asks, looking at him now. The ferry is leaving the heads. Beyond the lights of the colony at Breaker Bay, dark cliffs stretch away.

'To see my brother. How about you?' What he really wants to know is what crime she committed in Japan.

The ship begins to lift and fall with the oncoming ocean swell.

She speaks English, a thrilling violation of the rules. 'I'm visiting friends. I lived there for eighteen months before I came to Wellington.'

Smiling in the dark, he says, 'I see.'

'I had a Kiwi boyfriend there.' She glances around. 'A big secret, yeah?'

'Really?'

'He broke it off,' she tells the darkness. 'He wanted to fuck sheep instead.'

Surprised and delighted, he laughs. He didn't think it was even possible for a Japanese woman to say something like that.

Her lips briefly form a sad clown's expression. Her eyes are expressionless and humorous for it. He likes her at that moment as a woman, not as a Japanese woman. She turns to him and steps closer. Her hand flies out and brushes something from his shoulder. 'Bye.' It's oddly endearing. Her hands return and she adjusts his lapel in a very familiar way. Brushes more dust that only she can see off his chest with her nervous fluttery fingers. He's getting excited. 'I'm too cold,' she says.

'You could just about fit inside,' he says.

She gestures quickly that he should unbutton the coat.

Turning away from her, his heart hammering, he unbuttons the coat, not believing she'll actually get inside. Then her hat is under his nose, her hard skinny body against him. 'Button up,' she says. 'Make an oven.'

The coat is big enough. If someone comes up on deck, he thinks, they won't see her. She slips up a hand and takes her hat off. Her hair is fragrant, wonderful, and very personal. The ferry rolls in the ocean proper as he feels her hand on his crotch, touching him through his pants. She finds the zip, releases his dick and runs her fingers lightly up and down the length of it. 'Let me out,' she says. He doesn't move. 'Quick, over by the vent.' He sees the spot, a bolt of darkness that will make them invisible from the top of the steps on the other side of the deck, and lets her out. In the shadow she takes her coat off and stuffs it under the rail. Unbelievably, she reaches up under her knee-length skirt and whips her knickers off. She's back inside the warm cocoon of his long coat. He frees his right arm. Inside the tent of the coat he feels her cool flat stomach; kisses her neck as he runs his hands up under her blouse. She's braless; her nipples are long and hard. She reaches back again. Then she frees her hands from the coat and steps up onto the bottom rail, booted feet apart. She is very wet. She reaches back, hangs her bum down a little and guides him; a push and he's sliding deliciously in. Heat. He's gripped tight. She pumps and grinds on him; her back is lithe, snake-like. Hanging from the rail, her entire weight seems to clamp and centre on his cock. He groans. The stars are high and cold. Diesel fumes thread the air. It feels so good. He's never been fucked like this, so expertly. She releases a drawn-out sigh. If anyone comes now, he thinks, we're dead. She groans and he feels himself starting to come. *We're dead.* She feels so good, and he pictures her removing her underwear, the flash of pussy. It seems a miracle as he comes. She arches her lean back, shudders and pushes down hard. Then she lifts herself off. He undoes the remaining button to free her and she lightly steps down from the rail. He shields her as she quickly dresses. Now it's done he has an overwhelming desire to get away from danger, from the spot and from her, to get to safety below deck.

'Ah, that was incredible, but . . .'

She nods. 'Bye, Teacher. Sleep well.'

After she's gone down the Tourist Steps, he waits. Thirty long seconds later, two Kiwi men come up. As he leaves, two Japanese tourists are ascending the Tourist Steps. A heavy-sea door swings on the deck below and he glimpses the back of a brown uniform, a soldier. He clatters down, shocked, and instinctively heads in the opposite direction. The soldier seemed to be hurrying away. Squeals come from above, from the tourists on the freezing, windy deck. It is suddenly a hive of activity up there and he feels very fortunate not to have been caught by Kiwis or Japanese. His relief quickly gives way to suspicion that the soldier he saw stopped access to the deck while Kurosawa was with him. She was meant to make contact with me, he thinks, but why? Why on earth would she fuck me? He stops and heads back, thinking he'll ask the two Kiwi guys if they were stopped from going up. But a soldier at the bottom of the steps requests his ID. The man takes his time examining it, even though it's green. He gives Chris's details into the radio on his shoulder, speaking excruciatingly slowly, spelling and re-spelling his name and address. They wait. The ID is cleared. The soldier looks through him, to the next passenger in the line wanting to go up to the top deck.

Apart from a dozen tourists taking photos of one another, there are two pairs of Kiwi men. He doesn't recognise either as being the pair he passed as he left. The dark spot by the vent where he and Miss Kurosawa did the deed offers much less privacy than he had thought. He approaches the nearest pair of young men, both clad in black jerseys and black jeans. 'Excuse me, guys, did you just get here?'

'What?'

The man who has replied is drunk and belligerent. Brought up on deck by his friend to calm down, Chris thinks.

'I mean, was the deck empty when you came up?'

'Why?'

Chris appeals to the other man, the more sober one. 'Did the guard hold you up for long down there?'

'What's your problem?' says the drunk. He goes to push Chris on the shoulder but his friend restrains him.

Chris looks away, keeps his hands in his pockets.

'Doug, give it a rest, will ya?'

'Fuck.'

'Yeah, mate,' says the sober one, 'there seemed to be problem with my ID but it's fine. Why?'

The drunk refocuses. 'What's your problem?'

'No problem.'

'I say there's a fucking problem.'

'Shhh, there's tourists here.'

'I'm looking for my girlfriend,' Chris says. 'Her ID's expired.'

'Oh.' The drunk looks shocked, like a bucket of cold water has been tipped over his head. 'Shit. That's no good, mate.'

He moves quickly through bright corridors shot with volleys of drunken laughter, the rows of New Hokkaido posters for the tourists protected by gouged Perspex, and machines vending Japanese cigarettes, junk food and soft drinks. A door swings open with the motion of the boat and startles him. Through a window he sees a group of lanky Russians in their green uniforms playing cards and drinking. Downstairs is calmer. The third-class sleeping area is thankfully dim and almost quiet. The engines are a soothing constant. He removes his shoes and steps onto the tatami-matted floor. The large room is covered with bodies lying under blankets and sleeping bags. A group of three young men are sitting up talking near the far corner, slurring their words. He notes that the spaces by the walls are taken as he selects one of the last orange vinyl and foam pillows inside the door. It's crowded and he has to tread very carefully. Halfway around the room, and seriously considering a return to the anonymity of the top deck, he sees a spot between two sleeping family groups that will accommodate him. He stretches out on his back. *I made it.* The ferry's engine hums through the mats. He's reasonably comfortable, warm, safe, and his mind does cartwheels. The thought of Miss Kurosawa makes him hard again. It was outrageous, unreal, and he decides that she set him up, that she made contact to establish a relationship and get information. Maybe she has to do what they tell her to avoid prison. His dick hurts so he lets it out, safely concealed by his coat. He returns to the flurry of activity on the steps as he was leaving, the soldier disappearing through the door, maybe taking Kurosawa to be debriefed? Or she's a bad girl and we were lucky not to get caught, he thinks, turning over, no nearer sleep. The room has quietened down to the one slurred conversation between the three young men in the far corner. As their muttering rises in intensity, he focuses to catch the content and hears the unmistakeable sound of a tape-recorder button being pushed. There's a quick squirt of sound; the button is pushed again more emphatically and a sonorous voice rings out.

'Now let me tell you something that any reasonable person has known for years. The so-called Co-Prosperity Sphere is actually a Co-Poverty Sphere. The occupation isn't economically viable for New Zealand or Japan . . .'

Voices around the room. 'Jesus Christ.'

'Give it a rest, mate.'

'C'mon, it's after midnight.'

Chris looks. The tape recorder is on the lap of a young man, one of three about his age.

'Hang on—' The cassette whirs. 'I'll just play this bit. You need to hear this. All of you.'

'We can fulfil our true potential—'

'Fuck.' The cassette whirs briefly.

The recorded voice is familiar, but Chris can't place it until someone says in reverential tones that it's Roger Douglas. The name is whispered again and again. Chris recognises the voice. Yes, it's Free New Zealand's fearless leader in hiding.

'Let him speak!' someone cries.

The volume is turned up, overriding the complaints. 'Let me tell you that we're more than a beef farm and skiing destination for our Japanese oppressors, much more than a New Hokkaido. We are *New Zealanders*, a proud sovereign nation. We can fulfil our—' Clunk, whirrr. 'I dream of a New Zealand railways run by and for New Zealanders. I dream of a New Zealand telecommunications company run by and for New Zealanders.'

'Yes,' says one of the drunks.

'I dream of New Zealand power companies run by and for New Zealanders.'

'Yes.' A couple more voices respond, affirming each point.

'I dream of warm and dry housing, of food in the bellies

of our children, of power that every New Zealander can afford. I dream of . . .'

Only one comment of many—'You want to be arrested?'—bothers the man with the tape recorder.

'Are you threatening me?' he asks thickly, turning the volume down. He's very drunk.

'No. I'm just saying if you play that in here you'll get arrested. You could get shot for that.'

'Ah, you guys love the fuckin' nips.'

'Go to sleep, mate.'

'Don't fuckin' tell me to go to sleep.'

'Stay awake then, but shut the fuck up, eh?'

Chris raises his head. A middle-aged Maori man is sitting up. His wife is trying to pull him down.

'You guys welcomed the invasion,' says another of the drunk three. 'Welcomed the end of the white colonists. Cheered when our statues were toppled.'

'You are out of linc, bro.'

'Now you're working with them,' says the drunkest. 'It's all about money for you.'

The Maori man says, 'My father died for this country, died fighting under the New Zealand flag.'

There's a large sudden movement, curses, a muffled scream. The young man swings wildly, well short of the middle-aged man who has also stood up. His two drunk friends are pushing two other Maori guys. Chris is far enough away that he doesn't have to move. He turns over and closes his eyes and hears a clean punch connect—*thock*. Shouts, bodies falling over other bodies, children and infants wailing, people yelling for quiet. Suddenly it is quiet, but for the infants. Peeking, he sees soldiers in the doorway, and, appallingly, hears the still-running tape recorder, quieter but still audible: '. . . more than a beef farm and skiing destination for the Japanese, much more than a New

43

Hokkaido. We are *New Zealanders*, a proud—' Mercifully, it is turned off.

A soldier yells in Japanese from the doorway: 'Whose is that tape recorder?'

The light comes on and Chris hides his head under his coat. It's a serious offence and he fears what will happen.

'You. Come here.'

'Me?' Also in Japanese.

'Yes!' There is fury in the soldier's voice.

He feels their presence, the fear as the soldiers enter the room.

'Is it yours?'

'Aahh!' Maybe the young man has been pulled to his feet by his hair.

'Is it yours?'

A blow and a strangled cry. Chris blocks his ears with his fingers but it doesn't stop him hearing the young man deny ownership of his tape recorder. He hears the man's friends deny knowing him, a blow with a baton, a sharp cry. Through gritted teeth the man admits owning the tape recorder and claims he's travelling alone. Chris sneaks a look. The man is marched out alone by two soldiers, his arm twisted high behind his back, blood streaming from his nose. The bright light reveals him to be about eighteen. It's possible he'll be thrown overboard for the cassette—soldiers hate the ferry run. The light goes out. A soldier says, 'Any more problems and I throw a grenade in.' It's not just infants and babies crying in the dark, adults are also sobbing and moaning. Chris cries too.

# Chapter 4:

# Crime scene

Although his brother's house is close to the port there is no pedestrian access through the tunnel, so he must wait on the train, which is inexplicably delayed and unheated, and doesn't pull out until shortly before ten. He wears sunglasses he bought from the ferry kiosk, and dozes. Many of the passengers are hungover, or seem to be, and when the train jerks into motion they remain asleep under the blankets and sleeping bags they used on the ship.

As the train enters the tunnel he feels a twinge of excitement, an echo of the sensations he felt as a boy going to stay with his near mythical older brother, when the tunnel was like the magic wardrobe in his favourite book. The dark would release a shiver of anticipation at the thought of the marvels that waited on the other side. The train would burst into a bright new world, the idyllic rural settlements of the Heathcote Valley, with their high, gabled, ornately tiled mansions and manicured farms.

When the train stopped he would be the only Kiwi to get off, usually the only person, as on such summer trips he travelled alone and in second-class with other unaccompanied children. The new friends he had made on the voyage would wave goodbye from the train. His favourites among them would be Lucy, Edmund and Susan. He himself, waving back, was Peter.

One of his brother's staff (an amazing thing in itself) had picked him up from the station the first time, but after that he walked the short distance alone down country lanes in the bright morning, towards his brother's mansion with its shutters thrown open and a friendly tendril of smoke rising from the chimney into the blue sky. The staff were like a second family: the stable master, the gardener, the head farmer. And each with their special tools and duties. He liked Amy best, the youthful cook who sang as she worked in the busy kitchen and always had something good to give him. His brother, master of all, all-powerful and loving, and frequently absent, was the golden lion.

The train clears the tunnel but no light explodes. It's his first winter visit and the sun is weak. No one waves goodbye as he gets off the train. The station is grey, concrete rather than burnished silver. His brother's daughter is dead.

Finding himself on the farm sooner than expected, he turns off the main drive to see Bison, Patrick's favourite bull and prize breeder. Black and heavy in the middle of the paddock, he's a sullen force, like a neutron star around which the pasture and fences slowly revolve. There was a time when Patrick could feed him by hand, but that was years ago.

The kitchen's back door is open. The sound of dishes clattering mingles with the familiar smell of fried bacon. It gives him a lift, a sense of homecoming that has been lacking. Amy has her back to him, bent over the sink. Leaning in the doorway, he says, 'Something smells good.'

'Oh.' Pink gloves blur as she scoots around the square workbench and gives him a sudsy hug. He hasn't grown any taller since his last visit but she seems shorter, her long blond hair has been cut to shoulder length, and when her smile relaxes he sees how tired she is. Only thirty-five now, she looks middle-aged. She raises her pink gloved hands on a hopeless gesture and hugs him again. She feels sad. 'Patrick's out,' she says. 'How was your trip?'

'Up and down.'

'Were you sick?'

'No.'

'Tea or coffee?'

Chris notices a child's colourful drawing stuck to a cupboard. An adult has written *Amy* in English and katakana beneath a smiling figure with red earrings and pink gloves.

'Um . . .'

Amy follows his gaze to the drawing. Tears fill her eyes. 'I never had children, you know, but Sarah was like a daughter to me. It's just unbelievable.' Her eyes flare. 'What kind of monster could do such a thing?' It's not a rhetorical question, he realises. She expects a helpful answer from him.

'We'll find out who did it and they'll be punished.'

She turns away and fills the kettle. 'Things will never be the same.' When she turns back, her eyes are streaming. 'Oh, Chris, she looked asleep. Like she'd wake up and take my hand and I'd lead her out of that horrible place, that fridge-room at the hospital. But when I touched her she was so cold. It just broke my heart to leave her there, all on her own. She should be here, Chris, at home where she belongs, but they won't release her. And the funeral's been moved again, to Thursday.'

'Amy, I won't be able to come. My job . . .'

'Oh, yes, that's okay, dear, I understand. It's just that no one seems to be able to come. Oh, and she was just the sweetest little girl.' She takes a deep breath and seems about to break down.

'I'd better see Chiyo,' he says hurriedly, knowing he'll break down along with her if he stays any longer. 'I'd better tell her I've arrived.' He hugs her again.

She gathers herself, tries to smile. 'Okay, love. She has a guest, an old friend of Patrick's from Japan, who'll be glad to see you.'

He knocks on the door of the main room.

'Yes?' In Japanese. It's Chiyo and she sounds displeased.

He slides the door enough to reveal his face. She is sitting on the floor at the tea table opposite a huge and spectacularly fat Japanese man, certainly a former sumo wrestler. He reminds Chris of Bison: a dense object around which the room is held suspended. He is a man of great strength, but a man his brother must have beaten.

'Sorry. Please excuse my interruption,' he tells Chiyo. 'I couldn't wait to express my deepest condolences.'

'Oh, Chris,' she says, leaping lightly to her feet, a butterfly compared to the brooding mountain across the table. Her little hands take one of his and enclose it tightly. 'Thank you for coming so soon. Please come and have some tea, you must be tired.'

He wants to hug her, hold her properly, but she has company. 'I came as quickly as I could to be of help in any way I can.'

'Thank you. Please come in. This is Mr Kobayashi,' she says, 'an opponent of your brother's. He's an old friend. This is Chris Ipswitch, Patrick's only brother.'

The name is not familiar. Chris decides not to enquire what Mr Kobayashi's wrestling name was because his face is unfamiliar and he may not recognise it. The ex-wrestler nods respectfully.

'My fighting name was Noble Dawn,' he says.

Chris makes the connection. 'Ah, yes! It's a great honour.' He has put on a lot of weight since his retirement, to the point that his face has altered, but Chris can see the man before him in the famous pictures and videos now. He was the only wrestler to win the majority of his bouts against Patrick, and their fights in Japan rank among the all-time classic sumo bouts. Chris is moved by the great man's presence. Humbled, he bows low. 'Thank you so much for coming, sir.'

Noble Dawn nods once.

Chiyo pours tea studiously from the best set of china. He feels the energy in the room subside and reform.

'I was just telling Mr Kobayashi that the police still haven't interviewed me properly. They haven't come or even called. Patrick has gone to speak with them.' She refills the ex-wrestler's cup, which looks like an eggcup in his voluminous hand.

Chris allows this information to settle. If the police won't investigate, he thinks, the murderer must be Japanese. He's wondering how to frame this obvious conclusion when Noble Dawn says to Chiyo, 'Do you have incriminating evidence to give the police?'

'No. I saw nothing.'

'You said you were with a friend.'

'Yes, Mrs Kondo, the mother of a three-year-old, one of Sarah's playmates.'

'Did she see anything?'

'No.'

'Where was her child when it happened? Maybe the child saw something.'

'A man in black. A man with no face.'

'Did the child witness the—'

'No. The man frightened her. She ran away, but not to us, unfortunately. She hid in a fort.'

'Mmm.' Noble Dawn blinks with exaggerated care.

'Sarah was out of my sight for two minutes.'

Chiyo is about to cry and Chris expects Noble Dawn to drop the matter, but he continues.

'You told the police this?'

'Yes.'

'You have nothing to add.'

'No.'

'Then Pa-ta-rick-u should come home.'

'Yes.'

'I'll come back and see him. Talk to him.'

Chiyo sniffs. 'Thank you.'

'Please remember me kindly.' He places his teacup on the tray and claps his hand twice. His assistant appears and Noble Dawn places his meaty knuckles on the tatami mat, holds his weight on his forearms in order to uncross his feet, then straightens up with a burst of power. He's as tall as Chris and twice as wide. The assistant is there not so much to hold him up, Chris thinks, but to break or direct a fall. Noble Dawn bows slightly and then walks slowly away with heavy dignity, escorted by Chiyo like a tug leading a battleship out of port.

She returns sooner than he anticipated and is sitting almost before he realises it. He can see she wants to continue formally. It's not what he wants but he can understand the attraction of ritual in a time of crisis.

'He was my husband's greatest opponent,' she says. Her chin quivers and he guesses she is grateful. 'It's a great honour he should visit here.'

'Yes. Patrick will be sorry to have missed him.'

'Yes.'

'He has changed,' Chris says politely, referring to Noble Dawn's bulk. 'I didn't recognise him at first.' Ex-wrestlers typically lose weight upon retirement. Patrick is down to about 180 kilos from his fighting weight of 270.

'Yes. He retired early through injury. Too early, he told

50

me. He said he still eats like a wrestler.'

Silence. He sips the green tea.

'It's a very hard time for you,' he offers.

'Actually, the last three years have been hard.'

'Sorry, I didn't know.'

'Yes. People stopped calling. Japanese and Kiwi. He thought it would pass but it didn't. And now even Sarah's funeral must be a secret.'

'I'm sorry I can't be here for it.'

'We understand.'

A long silence. Chris wonders if he is at fault for failing to notice the isolation they have experienced and ends up feeling annoyed at her continuing formality. He realises she has always been basically formal with him. They speak Japanese and she is his elder. Her grief will not be fully shared with him, he realises, and she will expect the same self-control from him.

'Perhaps there is some small consolation in the end of your isolation,' he says sourly, hoping to shake some emotion out of her.

'Yes.' Her instant agreement shocks him.

She looks down.

So the farmer's daughter liked the bright lights, he thinks, then lost her status as the wife of a celebrity and found herself in a mansion she couldn't show off. There's always been something cold about her, something inscrutable in her doll-like face. He stares at the painted teapot and struggles to control himself. He doesn't like her. He doesn't trust her.

'I'm going to ask you a difficult question,' he says.

'Yes.'

'It will be hard for you, but I want to see where Sarah died. I need to know the mechanics of what happened. Once these basic and foolish questions have been answered I will be able to begin the grieving process and help my brother through his own grief.'

'You make a difficult request.'

'Please indulge me. I feel I cannot rest until I see for myself the scene of this tragedy.'

'Yes. I understand.'

'Please forgive me for suggesting that you show me as soon as possible.'

'Yes. Let me change.'

Ten minutes later he is following her white Toyota Star in the old Mazda hatchback with no handbrake. He expects her to pull over at the local park, but she continues on and he remembers that it happened in Hagley Park. She drives cautiously and as they approach Christchurch his anger subsides. Patrick's oft-repeated request comes to mind: that he move in with them at the farm and work in the lucrative tourist industry catering to the Japanese who come to the Southern Alps to experience New Hokkaido. Now he's not playing rugby, the offer is a lot more tempting. It feels like he should be with family more than anything else now. By the time they reach Hagley Park, he feels sorry for Chiyo, and has decided it was honest of her to suggest that Sarah's death wasn't all bad, that maybe there is some genuine tiny crumb of consolation in it. That's what I want from her, he thinks—more intimacy—and I got it. She parks under oaks by the Avon and he pulls up nearby. She removes her white driving gloves, checks her make-up in the car mirror, and she's off. He follows twenty metres behind to a large playground. He's been here several times as a kid himself and with Sarah. There are a few children and parents scattered about—Japanese and Kiwis fastidiously separate—wrapped up in scarves and hats. The paddling pool has been drained for the winter. The whole area is encircled by a thick and neatly maintained hedge that acts as a windbreak. A Japanese woman runs up behind Chiyo. Surprised, he almost shouts a warning, but Chiyo spins around as her name is called and submits to an embrace. The prolonged contact irks him; he's never been a recipient of such affection from her. But he can see that Chiyo is uncomfortable as he draws nearer. She's politely but desperately trying to disengage.

The woman says, 'I'm so sorry. She was a beautiful child.'

Chiyo is turning red-faced with vexation, and he's intrigued as to why she should be so allergic to this woman. The woman looks puzzled. She turns and sees him.

'This is Chris, Patrick's brother,' says Chiyo.

The woman disguises her surprise well. 'Good morning. I've heard so much about you. I'm very sorry for your loss.' She waits for Chiyo to introduce her but Chiyo seems paralysed. 'I'm Mrs Kondo,' she says.

A child of about three yells excitedly from a swing. 'Where's Sarah?'

He realises Mrs Kondo is the friend Chiyo had claimed to be with when the murder happened, and this is her little girl, who supposedly saw the murderer, the black man. He stares at Chiyo, who stands rigidly.

'Where's Miss Sarah?' shouts the little girl.

Mrs Kondo is mortified. 'I don't know what to tell Hana,' she says softly in response to the dismay etched on Chiyo's face. 'I'm not sure she'll understand. I'm very sorry. Please forgive me.' She scuttles back to the swing, calling, 'Come on Hana, I'll buy you some lemonade.'

'Yay!'

'What have you done?' he hisses at her.

She stares at the ground. 'We can't talk here.'

# Chapter 5:

# Johnny Lennon in jail

He follows the white Toyota Star to the main road. When Chiyo pulls out into the traffic he has to wait. She's a hundred metres away with half a dozen cars between them when she turns left through an orange light rather than straight ahead for home. 'Bitch!' he yells. He beats the steering wheel as he pulls out and follows her. 'You fucking Jap bitch!' He goes to make the turn and is stopped by a red light. He yells for as loud and long as he can, unexpectedly combusting in blind rage. 'Aaaaaaahhhhhh!' He bludgeons the air in the small car with his voice. 'They're all fucking spies!'

Almost as soon as his fury seizes him, it's over. He becomes aware of beeping. The traffic is moving. A cry of 'Fuckwit!' stretches from a passing Toyota pick-up. Chris raises his finger. 'Fuck you,' he yells. The pick-up, a high-sprung four-wheel drive, stops at the next set of lights, another red, and Chris pulls up behind it. The man has a mullet and a black jersey. He stares hard at Chris in his rearview mirror and raises his middle finger. Already Chris is over it. I'm going to the police station to see my brother, he thinks, not fighting a stranger in the street over a traffic light. The bogan misreads Chris's lack of interest for fear. His door flies open and he lands heavily on the ground in steel-capped boots. Skinny-legged in tight black jeans, broad shouldered and hard-faced, he struts towards Chris with a curious bendy gait.

Chris picks him as an unfit second-five-eighth who has a tendency to run sideways. He locks his door and stares straight ahead as the bogan raps on his window.

'Wind that down, faggot, or I'll fuckin' break it.'

The light goes green and a horn sounds. For half a second Chris considers opening his door hard on the man, then picking him up and carrying him across the road to dump him over a low garden wall; instead he swerves up onto the pavement and around the pick-up.

More horns and yells. He catches a glimpse of the bogan jumping behind the wheel and setting off in pursuit. 'Good,' he says to himself. He will lead the bogan to the police station and Patrick. In his rearview mirror he sees the pick-up swerving out from the line of traffic to pass, aborting, swerving out again, desperate to catch up. The bogan's about fifty metres behind when Chris sees the large Rising Sun and a lesser New Hokkaido flag above the imposing stone structure of the police station. There's a car park directly out front. He gets out and watches the bogan drive past slowly with his window down.

'Chicken-shit fucking faggot,' the man says.

Chris blows him a kiss. The tail lights flare as the man stops dead in the middle of the road. As Chris turns up the wide flight of steps in front of the station he hears another angry voice.

'What the fuck are you doing? You can't just stop in the middle of the fucking road, mate?'

As he enters the building, a policeman comes in behind him. Having seen what happened in the street, he says,

'Keep your petty disputes out of here.'

'Is murder petty?' Chris asks him.

'Usually,' the policeman says angrily.

Chris's temper flares again. 'Even if it's Japanese blood that's spilled?'

The policeman raps his fist on Chris's forehead. Spots of coloured light appear. It's the first time he's been struck that way since high school. The spots quickly fade. 'I have information about—'

'Silence!' barks the policeman.

'—a murder—'

Bang. More spots.

'Throw this dog in the pen!'

His arms are pinned as he's marched quickly across the lobby, past the desk, into the corridor leading to the cells. The policeman yells into his ear: 'Who gave you the right to speak? Who gave you the right to speak of Japanese dead?' A blow from a club on the back of his calf fells him. Blazing pain. Three or four men are kicking him. He curls into a ball. The attack is brief. Hauled to his feet, he is dragged a few steps to a cell and dropped inside. The door slams and a key turns. He springs up on his good leg and yells through the bars, 'I have information about the murder of a Japanese citizen!' But the police have already gone. 'Patrick? Can you hear me? It's Chris!'

'Hi, Chris,' comes a jeering voice from a nearby cell. 'Thanks for dropping by.'

The concrete cell features a bucket. He sits on the cold floor and assesses his injuries. Thankfully, they won't prevent him from returning to work—if he can get on tomorrow night's ferry. A clatter of boots and shouting brings him gingerly to his feet. A young man in a red-and-black jersey is thrown into a cell a few doors down. He must be a spectator from the Canterbury–Otago match at Lancaster Park. Chris

56

anticipates he'll be the first of many to be brought in the back entrance after separation and softening up. He's right. A steady stream of fans are brought in. Many go quietly but still there is yelling, scuffling and shouts of protest in the corridor and occasionally the flurry of blows and cries that herald a beating. Some arrive unconscious. As night falls they keep coming. One man begins to shout from his cell into the corridor that New Zealand is for New Zealanders. A stampede of boots and a cell door crashes open. Dull thuds ensue, and within seconds he's screaming, 'Please sir! Please sir!' in English, unwillingly spurring the beating to greater heights. 'Speak Japanese!' they yell. 'Yes! Yes!' he cries in English and falls silent. The beating goes on for a while longer, a terrible sound, and Chris grimaces as he imagines the damage inflicted to soft tissue and brittle bones. It makes the large, swollen bruise on the back of his calf feel minor.

As the cells continue to fill he sits in the corner and faces the door, expecting it to burst open any second. He thinks of Chiyo as cold radiates through his coat from the floor. A daughter of one of the neighbouring gentleman farmers who was an exporter by trade, she had taken a little job helping in Patrick's stable because she loved horses and her father wouldn't get her one. Her father, a huge sumo fan, enjoyed the arrangement. She ended up moving in to take care of the horses full-time. A very unusual thing indeed for a Japanese woman to live under a Kiwi roof, particularly if it had happened all at once, but over time, the odd night here and there becoming two nights, three nights, made the arrangement possible. The fact that she's plain would have helped, Chris thinks. A plain girl who loved her job with the horses, she was just one of several staff and helpers in a big and prosperous house. And Patrick was away fighting in Japan for most of the year. Chris remembers seeing Chiyo kiss her brother goodnight on one of his summer visits when he was about sixteen. He was shocked and yet, upon reflection, it seemed natural given their affectionate relationship. To see a Japanese woman in such a personal role was very surprising, but he made sense of it as another example of his brother's power. He wasn't allowed to tell anyone at school about her though, and their relationship was never publicly announced. Rumours that Patrick, the Pan-Asian Champion and a source of great pride for many New Zealanders, was 'fucking a Jap', or even better, 'fucking Japs'— plural—was another manifestation of his power. The Kiwi was on top and giving it to the Empire on all fronts. But the persistent rumours of a baby that came later changed everything. That was different. That meant a loving relationship with the enemy and the reaction to that was disgust. It was a betrayal so great that Patrick's entire career was retrospectively condemned. He'd been out for himself all along, not for New Zealand. All he was good for was pushing other big men out of a ring. That had shocked Chris.

Sitting on the cold floor of the cell, he thinks about betrayal, about the family Chiyo betrayed by having a child out of wedlock with a native. He doesn't know much about the consequences other than that her father disowned her. He doesn't know much, he realises.

As the night drags on and the beatings continue he worries that he's been singled out for special treatment, that they don't want him talking to a cellmate before he is disappeared. He feels powerless. If the Imperial Japanese Army wants his silence, he knows he will be silenced. The occupation will continue without him. Many people disappear every year. People he once knew, people he admires, like Johnny Lennon, who died in police custody in 1972 directly after the bootleg gig released as *Live in Levin*. Some of the soldiers who can be heard yelling in the final track, as the band is arrested amid howling feedback, would have been among those who beat him to death that night. Of all things to cry about, Chris thinks bitterly as tears well up, I should cry about that. He can't help himself. They put out a bright light, he thinks. A light that big, and they snuffed it out like a candle. What hope do I have?

Time passes. Something moves in the corner. A rat, he thinks. But it's the prone figure of a man. He hasn't been alone after all. He's had company all along, companionship. The dark figure stirs, as if tender. His head, pooled in darkness, is like a black-and-blue pumpkin. One eye, hanging from a tendril of nerve, retracts—zip—like spaghetti into pursed lips, and the eye returns neatly to its socket. 'Where's me fuckin' glasses?' says the man, in a resonant voice. 'Ah, there you are.' He sits up. Granny glasses gleam. His terrible head injuries and swelling are gone. His face is smooth and neatly moustached. The pattern on his psychedelic shirt slowly rotates. 'What's eating you, brother?'

Chris knows he can trust Johnny. It's a relief to have someone to talk to. 'I want to help my brother but things are spiralling out of control. I'm losing it. I fear I'll lose everything.'

'You can help your brother, brother, by keeping a lid on things for a start. You're normally very good at that, Chris.'

'I know, Johnny. Maybe it's because I don't usually engage with this fucked-up country. I keep my head down and work hard. Try to get ahead like Patrick did, you know.'

'You don't get where Patrick did by keeping your head down. He was the Pan-Asian sumo champion for five years, made Grand Champion, and is the only white man to even get in the top division. Look, forget that for now. He needs your help, for once, so help him. He wants to know the truth about his daughter's death. Rightly or wrongly, that's what he wants.'

'Did Chiyo kill Sarah?'

'It's unlikely.'

'Should I revisit the crime scene and look for clues?'

'And find a cigarette butt, a rare brand of cigarillo, a stiletto shoe print, sunflower seeds. A pair of bagpipes with a label saying—' Johnny adopts a high feeble-minded voice— 'These belong to Tumble Starkers, 23 Haggis Heights, Christchurch, the South Island, New Zealand, the Southern Hemisphere . . .' Chris feels mocked and uncomfortable, but Johnny smiles and puts him at ease. He holds up his packet to show he's down to his last cigarette, and lights it. Chris has three left. Johnny leans over and lights his for him with a cold blue flame from the end of a fingertip. 'It wouldn't hurt to have a look at the crime scene. You might get a hunch. Or a hump.' Johnny arches his back and leers, brandishes claw-like hands, and Chris can't help laughing. Johnny straightens up, instantly calm and serene. 'The thing to remember is that no one's going to do this for you. You'll have to go out and talk to people who don't want to be talked to. You'll have to ask questions that people don't want to answer. It'll be tough, the toughest thing you've ever done, Chris, but you can do it. I believe in you.' He starts to shimmer. 'And keep your head down, for Chrissakes.' His parting smile warms the cell long after he's faded.

Chris is woken by the sound of a heavy key turning in the lock. 'You'll be late for work,' says the policeman. He doesn't smile but has a humorous face.

'Thank you. My alarm didn't go off.' Chris cautiously stands and puts weight on his sore leg. To his relief, it's okay, and he's touched to feel the soldier's hand on his back in a friendly gesture. It reminds him of his dream of Johnny Lennon. Never has he had such an intense dream. It felt more like a vision, and he feels blessed somehow.

At the front desk he is processed formally and efficiently.

He is advised that his ID has been downgraded from green to orange. He asks the officer if his brother was at the station. The man consults a list and shakes his head. 'I suppose my car's been towed. It was out the front.'

'Possibly.'

Chris is strangely hopeful as he walks across the lobby, but the Mazda hatchback has gone.

# Chapter 6:

# The kindness of strangers

No one answers the phone at Patrick's house so Chris decides to retrieve the car by public transport. He rides a tram out to the last stop in Shirley and walks for ten minutes as per the directions on the tow company's business card. The tired, single-storey small businesses he passes—auto and farming gear specialists, the occasional kitchen and mirror showroom—are all customer-free, and unexpectedly comforting. Their sober interiors remind him of the safe and satisfying routine of the classroom.

One solitary button remains on his coat. He must return on tonight's ferry to be back in time for work or he'll lose his job.

A dog begins barking on the other side of a long corrugated-iron fence crowned with barbed wire. The invisible dog follows him down the fence until he comes to the entrance, where its barking takes on a whining, imploring note. The alarm has worked. A large man of about fifty with a walrus moustache and a shaved and notched head stands at the ready behind the counter. Built like an ex-Number Eight, he radiates a hard man's hostility. Although it's cold he wears a T-shirt. His powerful arms are clotted with filled-in and transformed old blue tattoos that hint at shifting allegiances. Chris senses that he fights often and usually wins, and that these victories are a source of pride and enjoyment for him. Not a team player.

'Yep,' the man says.

'Morning. I've come to get my car.'

'Which one's yours, mate?'

'The orange Mazda hatchback.'

'Rego?'

'Don't know.'

'Where was it, mate?'

'Outside the police station.'

'Right. Want a cup of tea, mate? Some toast?'

'That would be great.'

'Come through.'

The man, wearing shorts as well despite the weather, leads him into a small dirty kitchen decorated with pictures of naked Kiwi women. He directs Chris to a Formica table with three chairs. The jug boils quickly.

'What do you want on your toast?'

'Vegemite, please.'

He puts a teacup on the table in front of Chris. 'There you go. Black tea only I'm afraid.'

'Cheers.'

The man puts four slices of white bread in the toaster, sits down across from Chris, leans against the wall and lights a cigarette. 'Want one?'

'Thanks.'

'No charge for the tow, mate.'

'That's very kind of you.'

'Free New Zealand, mate.'

'Cheers.' Chris raises his chipped and stained tea cup in salute.

'What they keep you for?' The toast pops and the man gets up.

'I went to . . . my niece was murdered and I had some information to give them. They didn't want to know and I said the wrong thing.'

'There you go, mate.'

'Thanks.' The pile of toast on top of everything else releases a flush of gratitude. Touched, he nearly raises his trousers to show the man the injustice of his bruised calf.

'The police are fucking useless. Who killed your niece?'

'I don't know. Maybe . . . maybe the authorities.'

'Authorities? You from around here, mate?'

'No, Wellington. My brother's here.'

'Why would the Japs want your niece dead? What's your brother done?'

'He's the sumo wrestler the Night Train.'

The man jumps up and refills the jug. 'With respect,' he says as he sits down again, 'your brother fucked off a lot of people.'

'Yeah.'

'More tea?'

'Thanks. Do you think Free New Zealand might have done it?'

'Not Free New Zealand. I'm a member, as you might have guessed. I was more militant in my younger days, but I think Free New Zealand's on the right track now. The way out of this is political. Appeal to the Yanks and the Aussies. That's the conclusion I've come to. But there are still radical groups out there. You need to talk to them. There'll always be someone dumb enough to let something slip.'

'How can I contact them?'

'Stay right there.'

The man returns a minute later. A skinhead of Chris's age is with him. His blue overalls are unzipped to the waist and the empty sleeves hang behind him. Tautly muscled, a weightlifter, he wears a black singlet around which can be seen many religious tattoos: crosses, a depiction of the Sermon on the Mount, the miracle of loaves and fishes.

'This is Jock. I'm Doober, by the way.'

'Chris.' He stands and shakes Doober's hand. Jock doesn't respond to Chris's outstretched hand; he makes a show of carefully wiping his hands on the rag he brought in.

'Chris is a friend of mine,' says Doober.

Jock blinks to acknowledge this. 'What's up?' he says.

Doober leans back on the bench and crosses his bare arms and legs. He seems happy.

'My niece was murdered a few days ago in Hagley Park,' Chris says. 'She's the daughter of the Night Train.'

Jock fires a look at Doober and stops wiping his hands. Chris sees that Jock's suspicions about him are hardening into dislike.

'She's half Japanese,' Chris continues. 'The police won't tell us anything.'

'He got locked up for the night just for asking questions,' Doober tells Jock.

'Do you think a Kiwi could have done it?' Chris asks.

'Could've, mate,' says Jock.

'I think he means to ask if the organised resistance would make that kind of hit,' says Doober.

'Could do. Half Jap. That's fucked up.'

'He means did you guys do it?' says Doober.

'No,' says Jock.

'Did you talk about it?' says Doober.

Jock's face wrinkles as if something stinks. 'Yeah?' He turns to Doober and his face says, Where's this going?

Doober is enjoying the interrogation. 'Was it tabled as a possible mission?'

'Nah, mate. Not that. Not *us*.'

'Thanks, Jock.'

'Yeah.' Jock turns and struts out. The three ends of a tattooed cross poking out from his singlet indicate a crucifixion scene covering his entire back.

'Could be a rogue unit,' offers Doober, 'but they couldn't organise a piss-up in a brewery. Then there's the Lord's Angels, the outfit Jock's unit was basically at war with a while back. They're out of Wellington. They went back there.' He grins.

'I've heard of them.'

'I could give you an address in Wellington but you'd need some balls to see those guys about this issue. They're very, um, *racially orientated*.'

'You think they might have done it?'

'It fits their style: easy target, non-military.'

Chris stands. 'Thanks for your help, Doober.'

'No worries mate. Sorry about your niece, eh. I'll get your car and that address and you can be on your way.'

He heads south via New Brighton to avoid the CBD, intending to go straight back to the farm. Traffic is sparse and the lights all go his way. He hopes Patrick is at home and not out trying to find him. He passes a phone box; it's too good to resist. But when he brakes, the pedal goes straight to the floor; there's nothing there. Eighty metres ahead and approaching fast is a four-way intersection. A single car has stopped at the red light, a Toyota ute. He goes to change down and the engine graunches loudly; it won't go. The oncoming lane is clear so he swerves into it, back and forth, to buy a second of time; tries to chop down again. It goes, the engine screams, and he tries second. He hits the horn, tries to chop down again; it won't go. He knows not to hit an immoveable object such as a tree or power pole but something that will give. It has to be the back of the pick-

66

up. He honks and swerves again to gain a microsecond. He manages the chop down to second just before he backends the Toyota. His head hits the windscreen, his shoulder hits the door and he's on the road. There is broken glass. The pick-up comes to a rest across the intersection. The light turns green. He gets up. I'm okay, he thinks, touching the tender spot on his forehead. I could be dead.

'What the fuck?' The driver of the pick-up is looking back, out of his window. For an awful moment Chris thinks it's the bogan from yesterday, but it's not; it's another bogan. This one's older, with a short bushy beard. When the man's feet hit the road they are in jandals rather than steel-capped boots. The lights have changed again and traffic is running between them. He shouts across the road, 'What the fuck do you call that, mate?'

Chris sees the ute has no obvious damage. He holds up a hand. 'Sorry, mate, you okay? Brake failure. My foot hit the floor, nothing there.'

The man seems to slump a little. He circles his shoulders, mutters into his beard and looks for a break in the traffic. Chris is relieved he won't have to disarm him. He puts the little car in neutral, turns the wheel and begins to push it to the side of the road. The man's arrival is signalled by a lightening of the weight.

'Brakes failed?'

'Yeah. I went to stop to use that phone box up the road. Lucky I took my foot off the gas back there, I suppose.'

'Yeah, it could have really hurt.'

'Ha. Sorry man.'

'Nah, nah, glad you're okay, mate.'

The Mazda is parked and Chris feels a lump growing on his head where it hit the window. 'Is this kind of brake failure common?' he asks the man.

He breathes deeply and exhales. 'I wouldn't buy a Mazda,

personally. You usually get a warning with brakes though. If the lines have been cut they'll feel sluggish before they fail.'

'Right.' The car drives like a brick at the best of times and Chris is unsure whether he used the brakes this morning before they failed.

'I'd tow you, mate, but you don't have brakes.'

'I think someone's tried to kill me.'

'I don't know about that, mate.'

'Where can I find the brake lines? I want to see if they've been cut.'

'On a Mazda?' The man kneels in front the car and checks the road surface. Finding it clean, he turns on his back and wriggles underneath. 'Yeah. Mmmm.'

A police car pulls up, apparently summonsed by a member of the public.

All I need, Chris thinks. The police are often Settlers who have come to the end of their first probation period. They usually resent the job and are quick to anger. Worse yet are the Koreans, who tend to take out their frustrations with the Japanese on Kiwis. The officers climb out of their car and put on their peaked hats. They're Japanese and bored. He fears his recent stint in the cells will give them an excuse to throw him inside again. Because the man is under the car looking at the brakes, Chris can bow respectfully.

'Yes?'

'Sorry, my brakes failed,' Chris says in Japanese.

They see the bogan's legs poking out under the car and their eyes widen.

'I'll need spanners and a torch, mate,' comes his muffled voice.

The officers laugh. They laugh again, and Chris sees the funny side too. The man wriggles out and sits up to see what's happening.

'They thought I'd run you over,' Chris tells him in Japanese. The man leans his head back and laughs as well.

There is a mirror in the waiting room at the A&E and as he paces the empty room he glimpses the alarming lump growing on his forehead. It's the size of half a squash ball now and he can feel its presence, an awful jiggle, as he walks. He had initially rejected the offer of a lift to hospital but the police had insisted and even dropped him off. And now, as the headache kicks in and the lump continues to grow, he is grateful that he will be seen by a doctor and given painkillers. He tries a payphone.

'Chris?'

'Patrick. Thank God. I thought I was going to miss you. It's been crazy.'

Patrick speaks English. 'Where have you been?'

He quickly recounts his misadventures and his current location at the A&E, aware as he's doing so that he will have to broach the subject of Chiyo's lie and how much that will hurt his brother. 'Patrick,' he says, still unable to come to it, 'I have to go back to Wellington this evening or I'll lose my job, so I can't come to Sarah's funeral, but I can come down again next week, Monday and Tuesday. Also, about the car—'

'Chiyo told me what happened at the park.'

'I was coming to that, bro.'

Patrick sighs. 'She's told me everything. I think.'

'Good.'

'She says she lied about who she met, and the other kid seeing a "black man". No one saw anything. But everything else she said, the time Sarah was out of her sight, the locations, that's all the same. So she met a Japanese man. A man she is or was interested in. She says he's from Japan, a new regular at the kids' park on the weekend and they got chatting and started meeting on his lunchbreak without his kid there. I have two doubts about her story. One, she claims she let Sarah out of her sight for only two minutes. I think it was longer. And two, I suspect that this guy who was always at the fucking park may have set her up so the killer could get Sarah. Now, I could be wrong about him. Endo is his name and he's in Wellington next week on an education conference about Non-Business English. He's a big-shot in education apparently. He won't recognise you, so can you talk to him and check him out? If he's a cracker, I think we have a lead.'

'Okay. Endo. I guess if he refuses to talk to me, like on a face-to-face level if I "run into him", that's information in itself.'

'Exactly.'

Chris tells Patrick about the brake failure and concludes that they could have been tampered with at the police station or at the tow yard. 'The tow operator has a deal with the police,' he says. 'They have his card at the front desk, so—'

'I'll talk to him.'

Doober's motives are obscure to Chris; he suspects the man could be active against the Japanese and just as easily be killing for them, but he knows Patrick will come to an understanding quickly. The prospect is oddly thrilling. He gives Patrick Doober's address. 'He knows who I am, who you are, and about Sarah. If he claims ignorance, it's a lie. I can't believe I didn't get to see you.'

'Yes, you need to go straight to the ferry. Don't worry about Sarah's funeral, Chris. There's no point in losing your job and you can help by seeing this Endo character. I feel better for talking to you. Thanks for all your help.'

Chris glows. His chaotic weekend is instantly ordered by his brother's praise, rendered useful at a single stroke. 'No worries, man.'

'Stay out of jail next time!' Patrick manages to laugh.

Chris laughs as well. As he puts the phone down, he sees Doober standing at his front counter and Patrick's vast shadow darkening him and the wall behind him; Doober saying nervously, 'You're a big unit, mate?' Then the headache resumes and a new pulsing beat announces itself in the lump on his head. His name is called by the nurse.

# Chapter 7:

# Number four

Chris sighs deeply as he opens the door to his tiny Japanese-style one-room apartment. A gift from Patrick, he feels more grateful than usual for owning it and being able to live alone. He unrolls the futon in his living/sleeping area and lies down. The contusion on his forehead has begun to drain into his right eye, making it a dirty yellow-brown and squishy like rotten fruit. On the return voyage he went directly to the sleeping lounge and slept the whole way back, yet he feels he could sleep again. He wonders about Miss Kurosawa, about bringing her back to his apartment. It's a fantasy, he knows. The danger of being seen is too great.

Once, when very drunk, he brought a woman back to the apartment. It was closing time, 11 pm, mid-winter, and in retrospect he suspects she needed a bed for the night more than anything. She was an Auckland supporter and wore an Auckland scarf and a lot of clothes. Swaying, they had looked at his posters: Lennon, the Night Train. 'My brother,' he said and she laughed. And Colin Meads, the old-school lock who inspired him to run with the rugby ball one-handed. She hadn't recognised Meads. 'My other brother,' Chris said.

His memory of their fuck was that it went on and on. She left her socks and jersey on. Her dark hair spread out over the pillow. He was too drunk; the condom felt thick and barred any intimate sensation. Desperate to feel something he imagined her to be Japanese, the young racist teacher at work, Miss Sato, lying on the photocopier. It didn't help. He soldiered on, waiting for some feeling to develop, until she finally said, 'You're killing me,' and he stopped. She got up early in the morning and he let her go, feigning sleep. The apartment was exactly the same as before except for one thing: the insides of the windows were heavy with condensation, something that never usually happened. She was real after all.

The phone rings. It's Marty. He's heard about Sarah and expresses his condolences. He sounds sad. Says he has some weed. Chris explains he has to work in a couple of hours because he owes a colleague some classes. Marty says he'll pop around quickly.

Half an hour later Chris opens the door and Marty is standing there with his disappearing blond curly hair. Magician-like, he opens his hand to reveal a big unlit spliff.

'Jesus.' Chris hauls his friend inside before anyone can see.

'What happened to your face?'

'I banged my head just here on the inside of a car window. The dead blood or whatever is draining down.'

'Dead blood? Lucky you teach English not science.'

'Tea?'

'Thanks.' Marty drops the joint on the table. 'For you, Chris; might take the edge off.'

'Cheers. You know, I didn't get to see Patrick the whole time I was down there.'

'How come?'

'I got thrown in the cells for trying to discuss the case at the jail. Don't ask. Then my car got towed. I got it back and the brakes failed . . . hospital, ferry, home. The funeral's in a couple of days. I can't go.'

'Jesus. I'm sorry to hear that, mate.'

Chris sits down heavily at the table. He's aware of the time and his impending appointment with Masuda's wrath.

'You've been in the wars all right,' Marty adds.

'Yeah.'

'Three years old?'

'Yeah.'

'Jesus, there are some psychos out there. The country's fucked.'

'A funny thing happened in the cell: I had a kind of vision of Johnny Lennon. He said I should help Patrick. Like it was up to *me* to save him. It was weird. Very intense and realistic.'

'Did he say anything you didn't know already?'

'Um, not really.'

After looking gloomily at the floor for some time, Marty says, 'Did he mention dark-haired strangers? Going on a journey?'

For a chilling moment Chris suspects his friend knows about Miss Kurosawa, that his secret is out. But Marty couldn't know. And she has blue hair anyway. 'No?' he says.

'Be nice to just get on a plane and leave, wouldn't it?'

'Yeah.'

'Or steal a yacht or something.'

It's an old dream of theirs. Chris nods and thinks of Miss Kurosawa.

'Got time to cut my hair?'

'Eh? Your crowning glory? Your mum'll kill me.'

'We'll put it in a bag for her.'

'But I don't know how to use a curler and hot irons.'

'Very funny. Just do it like you do Bill's.'

Chris has clippers and every month, Bill, his old locking mate and the team captain, comes around for a number four and a beer and tries to convince Chris to quit his job and play rugby. The Japanese have made it mandatory that rugby teams be captained by Maori as part of their policy against former racist colonial masters. The result is that the official captain is not always the actual captain, and if a game gets niggly, refs will sometimes call in exasperation for 'the real captains, please'. They always know that Bill is the real captain.

'Sick of the piss-takes?' Chris says.

'Not really. I think I'll miss it.'

The truth will come out, Chris thinks. 'Do you want to watch?' he asks as he takes the clippers down from the cupboard. 'I'll cut it here but I can get the bathroom mirror.'

'No.' Marty takes his jersey and shirt off. He's a bit serious.

Chris holds the buzzing clippers above Marty's remaining blond curls, still thick at the back and sides. 'I can't do it. They're too beautiful.' Marty doesn't bite so Chris begins shearing. Marty catches a tumbling bunch of ringlets, looks at them, then lets them fall to the ground. It's a sombre haircut. It feels to Chris like a coming of age, a rite marking the end of Marty's childhood and passage into decades of work as a casual labourer in road gangs and construction. The result is jarring: Marty's hair has been such a big part of him. 'A number four,' Chris announces grimly as he turns off the clippers.

Marty runs an experimental hand over his head and goes to the bathroom. 'I'll get used to it,' he says when he returns a minute later, wet-faced from washing his head and neck.

Chris has swept up the hair with a brush and shovel and is about to drop it in the bin.

'I actually will give that to Mum,' Marty says.

'Right.'

'No, really.'

Chris tips the silky hair in a plastic bag.

'Thanks.'

'Don't tell her I cut it,' Chris says. 'She'll never forgive me.'

'I won't.'

A moment of heavy silence.

Chris ruffles Marty's scalp. 'I'll miss it, you know. Is there a special occasion?'

'We're going down on the ferry for the Wellington–Canterbury match. You know, big piss-up, lots of fights.'

'Shit, I'm working.'

'Word is there'll be a huge fight this time.'

'Yeah?'

'Yeah . . .' Marty runs his hand over his shaved head again, regretfully it seems. 'You know, with us being regional champs now. Few points to prove.'

'Right, yeah. Pity I have to work now,' says Chris. 'I would love to sit down with a couple of beers, some good music and a smoke this arvo.' He means it. The trip to Christchurch he could do without, though: the downing of beers until oblivion, and the punch-ups and the bullshit and the hangovers. And he senses Marty knows that.

'Yeah,' Marty says significantly. 'Shame.'

# Chapter 8:

# Contaminated

Misty curtains of rain sweep in from the north. Tin awnings drum; full drainpipes splutter and choke into pooling gutters. It's cold as well but he would like to extend his short walk past the Language Academy and continue for hours. He'd like to walk along the waterfront in the rain, go all the way to the Thistle Inn, where Johnny Lennon began playing as a teenager after running away from home in Levin, and have a quiet beer, but he can't. Climbing the wide flight of stairs towards the sentries at the entrance to his work, he wonders once again if it's best to avoid Masuda or simply get it over with.

He walks straight up to Masuda's desk and bows. 'Good morning, sir.' He's suddenly conscious that his ID has been downgraded from green to orange and feels the weight of fluid encased by skin around his eye like a manifestation of sin.

'Your face?'

'Sorry. A car accident, sir. My forehead struck the window and the swelling is draining into my eye.'

'Yes. A nasty bump.'

Chris is so surprised he says, 'Thank you.'

'It's a difficult time for your family. We're sorry about this accident in Christchurch.'

Chris bows again. 'Thank you, sir.' He's touched.

Masuda nods and his glasses flash a dismissal.

Only later does he wonder about Masuda's choice of the word 'accident'. He decides it's innocuous, a euphemism, and returns to feeling grateful.

Despite the unsettling sensation of weight on his face, more notable when he moves enthusiastically, accompanied by a feeling of seediness similar to a hangover, he enjoys the classroom, the resumption of order and the sensation of losing himself in work and doing a good job. The bruise makes his students sympathetic, and by the time the fluid has descended to make a yellow-and-brown ridge on his jawline in the early evening, staff and students alike are impressed by his dedication. At 8 pm when the principal gets up to leave, thereby releasing all the teachers, Chris asks Masuda if he can attend the conference on non-business English at the town hall the next day. He expects to have to ask three times, but Masuda tells him the entire English team, including himself, will be attending. Chris is happy. His plan was to gauge Mr Endo's reaction to him in a face-to-face conversation—which would have probably meant jumping out of an alley or following him into a restaurant—to see if his white face elicited any measure of disgust, but as basic as that plan was he knows it would have been ruined by his ghastly bruising, which would affect any person's reaction to him. It will be much better to sit and watch the man from the audience, listen to him talk and gain an impression of him that way.

Pleased at the prospect of being to be able to do what Patrick asked him, and pleased by Masuda's and his students' sympathy, he leaves work with a real spring in his step.

Miss Kurosawa comes to mind; she will be in his last class tomorrow after the conference. So good is his mood that he decides that's also a good thing.

The next morning, the roads around the town hall are closed for the education conference, blocked by soldiers with armoured cars and jeeps with mounted machine guns. Chris has never seen such heavy security. Helicopters troll overhead. Tour buses for those arriving from further afield are parked a couple of kilometres away on the waterfront and searched for bombs. All the fuss and threat of danger puts the teachers in a festive mood. While they are nodded through checkpoints, Chris must produce his ID three times and submit to three searches. His colleagues are so excited to see friends and acquaintances from other schools and academies that he manages to conceal his ID's new orange colour from them. The crackle in the air reminds him of the build-up to the Night Train's bouts in Tokyo, even though he only saw them on TV and the crowds and the venue and the sense of anticipation were so much greater.

The town hall is packed with teachers, maybe eight hundred, all in suits and formal dress. They sit in neat rows on tatami mats and cushions in front of the stage, buzzing excitedly. A chopper clatters overhead. Everyone feels important. Kerosene heaters placed along the walls have pre-warmed the room and are now off. He can see why the security is so tight: one bomb would significantly impact the Empire's educational programme in the lower North Island. Chris's is one of only half a dozen white faces in the hall, and the only one with extensive bruising. He's happy to sit down.

The first speaker confirms the unhappy fact that English has become the language of world trade, even in unlikely places such as Africa and South America. He talks about the importance of non-business English in business deals, which are often made on the golf course when dealing with US companies. He suggests that business in the US is about building relationships nearly as much as it is in Asia. Perhaps, he suggests, some trusted and properly educated native speakers would be useful? At this point Masuda pats Chris on the knee in a paternal gesture. Chris flushes at the extent of the compliment. Excited, even teary with gratitude, he bows his head where he sits. His future has become clear. It's on a vast golf course in the sun in America as a trusted and respected envoy. He knows he'd be good at it. He knows it. He feels that a secret path has been dazzlingly revealed.

Applause breaks out as Mr Endo, the keynote speaker, is introduced. *Are you a killer?* Chris wonders, doubtfully, as the slim figure walks to the podium. He's about Patrick's age, maybe in his early thirties, which is young to be the head of non-business English programmes throughout the Empire. The clear-faced man has prestige and power, a much different power from Patrick's: a power to organise ideas, and convince and coordinate people. Within seconds Chris decides he is not involved in the murder, simply because he's too busy. The Imperial Japanese Army would get someone else to play charming solo father in the park. His opening remarks are about New Zealand being the only colony in which English is widely spoken. He agrees that English is an asset for trade with the US and Australia, and that fluent and attractive native speakers could help facilitate business deals by providing social lubricant for the Japanese negotiators. There's a titter and Chris realises he means pretty women, maybe comfort women. He's gobsmacked. Masuda doesn't pat his knee again. As Endo drones on about the importance of the work the teachers are doing, Chris's embarrassment and disappointment slowly subside. Then his heart sinks as Endo moves on to the inferiority of English, its deficiency in articulating honour, its spiritual deficiencies and role in the cultural decadence of the West. The crowd nods enthusiastically. Chris nods as well, for Masuda's benefit. The chopper clatters overhead. Endo concludes that non-business English be taught to Japanese children only with the awareness that it is morally ambiguous at best and spiritually contaminating at worst. After prolonged applause it is announced that questions will be taken from the floor after a short break.

Chris gets Masuda a cup of tea and generally fusses over him, something he doesn't mind doing given the praise heaped on him by the tap on his knee, even though it was misguided and embarrassing for both of them. Endo is clearly very conservative and possibly arch-conservative, a man capable of blind hate. I'll catch the conscience of the king, he thinks. 'Mr Masuda.'

'Yes.'

'What should be done with a Japanese child morally contaminated by English?'

'Mmmm. I will ask Mr Endo.'

After the break, Masuda raises his hand and is honoured to be able to ask the first question from the floor.

'A good question,' Endo says, and there is a ripple of applause. 'The answer is to remove them from the toxic environment that has corrupted them and heal them with immersion in correct culture.'

More applause.

So if Sarah was contaminated by the English she learned, thinks Chris, what of the blood flowing in her veins? Was it an opportunity killing? Did Endo come across an unclean child at Hagley Park and take it on his own bat to remedy the situation? Just as a side project on his lunch hour, in the service of the Empire? If not, what was he was doing with

Chiyo? It seems to Chris that some pressure could be put on Endo—a married man, he assumes—to explain that.

While walking back to work with his colleagues after the conference, there is an animated discussion about the points the speakers raised. It is noted that some children at the Academy being taught non-business English are only five, and the inherent moral flaws of English are not being protected against at all. Would it be best to wait for an official policy announcement or begin to make changes to the curriculum already? Because his opinion can be given only if solicited, which is unlikely given the enthusiasm of the conversation, Chris's mind drifts to Endo and then to Miss Kurosawa. He expects she will be discreet in the classroom, whatever her motivation was for doing what she did. It was quite incredible, really. Quite incredible. Something he finds oddly endearing is the way she took her hat off after she'd climbed into his coat. The way she released the fragrance of her hair, and the warmth of her neck and body, seems to him a genuine and personal touch. It was romantic. Or, he thinks, was I getting carried away? It certainly set the ball rolling, anyway. At that point it had been clear that she wanted more than coat warmth. The chatter around him has stopped. He's been asked a question apparently. 'Mmmm,' he says, knotting his brow. 'I don't know.' The chatter resumes.

# Chapter 9:

# Women and history

At 4:55 pm, as the first of Miss Kurosawa's classmates arrive for the 5 pm lesson, he finds himself wondering what to do with himself, whether to write on the board or look busy at his desk. He sits down. Her appearance stops his breath like the visit of an apparition. Her eyes are blank yet humorous as she says, 'Good afternoon, teacher,' in slightly brazen English.

He stands and bows. 'Good afternoon, Miss Kurosawa.'

Tall and skinny like a girl, but with wide shoulders and a chest, she has a woman's elegance. She sits in her spot at the back of the left row, opens her book and adds, after a second's thought, 'What happened to your face?'

The rest of the class notice. 'Oh.'

'I was in a car crash. I hit my forehead'—he indicates where that is—'and the swelling has drained into my face.'

'Ooooh.'

Once everyone has arrived he explains his injury again then instructs the class to open their books to page twenty-three: Transport.

'Trans-port,' says someone thickly.

He reads a description of Tokyo commuting that involves a car, train and subway ride, then puts the class in pairs to discuss their commute to the Academy. They can talk about their longest and shortest commutes in the past as well. He walks around looking delighted at what he hears; in moments of silence he's never less than cheerful.

Miss Kurosawa looks up from her conversation with the woman at the desk in front of her. 'Teacher? Is it polite to ask someone if they have a car?'

'"Do you drive?" is better.'

'Do you drive?' she asks him.

'Yes,' he says. He pauses for a jangling moment. *We can fuck in my car.* 'That's correct polite usage. Do you drive?'

She nods. 'I understand,' she says.

His ghastly bruised face feels hot. He turns to the next group and inclines his happy head over their conversation.

The final seconds of the class beat like war drums in his chest. He bows, the students leave, Miss Kurosawa straggles. They're alone. He sits down at his desk to avoid an unusual display of body language should anyone look in.

'Hi, Hitomi,' he says and smiles as she comes to the desk. 'Hi, Chris,' she says, a little loudly he thinks. She's not a person given to smiling; it's more like lightning flashes cross her face. 'Park your car here at 11 pm on Friday night,' she says, pushing a slip of paper towards him. 'I'll get in the back door.'

'Yes. I will,' he says in Japanese, at normal volume, and stands emphatically. 'Thank you.'

Her face flashes again briefly and she's gone.

He has two days to get a Kiwi girlfriend and stand Hitomi Kurosawa up. Trouble, trouble, trouble, he thinks as he pounds up the road towards the misty summit of Mount Victoria the next morning, trouble, trouble, trouble. It's a huge violation. If they are stopped and found in a car together it will mean his disappearance. He will cease to exist. From the top of the mountain he sees nothing but mist and the steam he's blowing like a train. He turns back. Trouble, trouble, trouble. The problem with finding a girlfriend by Friday night is that he works from 5 to 11 pm tonight and tomorrow. His daily routine is running, then swimming or boxing at the gym. Running is solo. There are regulars at the pool but no one he fancies. The gym is male only. The mist thickens into drizzle. He thinks of the places women go in winter: shops, the library, movie theatres, the museum. To interrupt a woman without being drunk? Impossible. Or is it? He thinks of Emily again, the busty brunette with a long neck at the New Zealand Culture evening.

Showered and calmer, he rings Marty to find a contact point, but no one answers. He's relieved. Emily would have shot him down. He checks to see if he has the number of anyone else who was at the party. He doesn't. He knew he wouldn't. Again, a sense of relief. He rings his brother. While waiting for someone to pick up he remembers talking to Sarah on the phone: her high-pitched voice, careful but not precise, as she told him about a kite Daddy made for her, or her pet lamb Ewan. She liked to laugh and didn't need to know exactly why something was funny. The phone rings and rings. He misses her loving directness. Amy unexpectedly answers and her enthusiastic greeting makes him smile. She tells him Patrick has gone to see a mechanic—Dooby, she thinks—and he hears a metallic crash. Sorry, a pot lid, she says.

It's just as well Patrick is out, he thinks as he hangs up. Although he hadn't intended to mention Miss Kurosawa, she probably would have come up. In fact she would have. And the trustworthiness of a Japanese woman is a subject too close to the bone for his brother at the moment. He wants to give Patrick a break rather than aggravate him.

It's drizzling as he pauses on the steps beneath the Carillon. As if securing a girlfriend in the museum before 3:45 pm wasn't hard enough, he has the ghoulish remains of the black eye. He looks up the tower. The stone that appears sheer from a distance is deteriorating in places and needs to be replaced. The Carillon is the tallest surviving pre-invasion structure in Wellington and one of the very few remaining public monuments. The only old statues left are nymphs and cherubs on fountains. Yet the light for the Unknown Soldier still burns, partly because the Japanese venerate their dead ancestors, but mostly because the memorial serves as a reminder of the sacrifice the old colonial masters the English demanded of New Zealand. What is England doing now for her loyal colony who gave so many lives? asks the Carillon. Nothing. In 1943, with New Zealand well under heel, Japan issued a proclamation calling for common prosperity and wellbeing based on justice, respect for independence, sovereignty and traditions. Economic development would be accelerated on the basis of partnership, and all racial discrimination would end. The only requirement was that English be banned, along with the local press and radio, Western music and political parties, etcetera. He grinds his cigarette out on the wet step. Stop wasting time, he tells himself, and find a woman in the museum.

Of all the places to talk to a woman it seems to present the best possibilities: speaking is permitted, unlike in a library, and the exhibits inspire comment and conversation, unlike the clothes in a shop. But as the stone edifice of the museum comes into view under its three rising suns, ceremoniously guarded by soldiers with long bayonets fixed to their automatic weapons, he remembers that most Kiwis regard the history inside the museum as propaganda, and stay away. His mother, he remembers, was made apoplectic by the New Zealand history section. He must have been about eight. Her fists had clenched and her arms became rigid as if she were holding invisible skis.

Well, I'm here now, he thinks. It's 1:30 and he has a couple of hours. He makes for the Egypt section, by far the most popular exhibit in the museum. A class of uniformed boys and girls, aged about eight, chatter in Japanese before the mummy. The sound of children speaking Japanese is enough to reduce the older generations to tears sometimes, but Chris doesn't feel that pain. They can speak English at home now. It's been many years since the Imperial Japanese Army tried to stop that. The assistant teacher is a Kiwi. She's young, stocky, freckled, harassed and a little surly. The Japanese teacher asks for quiet and begins to pick some facts from the pamphlet she holds. The assistant teacher smiles briefly with her mouth at him. He's sympathetic. He knows the hoops she must jump through to work in education. When the teacher finishes her fact sheet, the class babble excitedly. Walking past, he'd like to say something encouraging to the assistant, but the teacher would hear so he nods instead.

The first panel of the World War II timeline, 1937, has a familiar black-and-white photo of happy Japanese soldiers posing on a steam locomotive. They've swarmed all over it for the picture. *After the Manchuria incident*, says the caption, *Japan was hurtled into war with China*. Just what Japan was doing in Manchuria in 1937 isn't mentioned. 1939: the fact that Japan and Nazi Germany were allies is not mentioned. He checks quickly along the wall. No, the Axis alliance between Japan and Germany never existed. He's had enough, but another school group arrives just as he's leaving. The Kiwi assistant teacher is tall and slender. Her hair is cut stylishly short and she has large eyes. Unlike the other assistant teacher she is relaxed and at ease. She's speaking Japanese with one of the kids, and hasn't seen him. She is light to Miss Kurosawa's darkness. I'll make a connection with her today and follow up tomorrow, he thinks. She's still oblivious to his presence and he feels like a predator, something dark and reptilian, as he follows her and her class into the Egypt room.

The Japanese teacher is middle-aged, short, and severe. Rather than paraphrase the pamphlet as the previous teacher did, she reads it to her class, word for word, to complete silence. The assistant teacher stands respectfully to one side, almost at attention, with one hand clasped over the other. She sees him and raises her eyebrows in greeting. It sets his nerves jangling. 'Yes?' the teacher says to him.

Surprised, he bows. 'Very interesting, Teacher,' he says. The children giggle uncertainly.

'Please continue to the next exhibit,' she tells him.

'Sorry.' Humiliated, he turns on his heel and walks straight out of the museum and down the steps until he reaches the Carillon, the monument to the dead, where he turns and heads back up. The soldiers on guard at the entrance flick their eyes at him. 'Forgot my notebook,' he calls cheerfully and strides back inside.

He positions himself at the end of the timeline, in the far left corner, and waits. His intention is to work backwards, anti-chronologically, and run into the assistant teacher when the class arrives and see if he can generate a spark. He realises he has a business card he can slip her. It's perfect: respectable and professional. Why didn't he think of it sooner? He waits at 1985, the last entry: New Hokkaido. It features a picture of the defaced New Zealand flag and a pool at Hanmer Springs with snowy mountains behind. All the faces in the steamy water are Japanese. *After the brilliant New Hokkaido advertising campaign by Tourism New Zealand, which included the re-launch of the national co-prosperity flag, record numbers of tourists are attracted to New Zealand to experience her beautiful mountains and hot springs. They can also enjoy beefsteak that is tenderer and less expensive than in Hokkaido itself.* Patrick once described Hokkaido to Chris as 'a frozen shithole'. A nervous hiccup of a laugh escapes him at the memory and echoes disconcertingly in the empty room. He moves down to 1984 and hears the patter of well-drilled little feet. The dragon who dismissed him collects her class at 1937 and reads the placard aloud: 'After the Manchuria incident, Japan was hurtled into war with China.' The assistant teacher avoids eye contact with him as he moves to 1973, The Oil Crisis: *Western business leaders conspire to create global fuel shortages and cause a humanitarian crisis.* The class moves to 1939; he moves to 1968: *Edmund Hillary climbs Mount Cook for the 50th time.* They'll meet in the 1950s, at the creation of the co-prosperity/New Hokkaido flag, and the posters of the era featuring it. What won't be mentioned are the fire bombings on the homes of the Kiwi artists who made the posters. He fingers his business card.

A child's clear voice pipes: 'Teacher, the young gentleman's going the wrong way.' Giggles again. He tries to ignore the comment but it's impossible; he feels the burn of the dragon's glare.

'Right to left!' she tells him, and the class giggles more certainly at the young man scolded for reading the wrong way, as if he were turning pages in English. He should know better than that! They laugh properly as he turns on his heel and walks out. This time he doesn't stop at the Carillon.

# Chapter 10:

# Working the phone

On Thursday Miss Kurosawa is very professional in class. She focuses on her work and interacts with her classmates. Like the two other Settlers, the males, she's articulate and sensible when it comes to group and class work. Murder of a Japanese and treason are capital offences. Settlers, he has heard, have committed crimes of an 'anti-social nature', such as fraud, theft, drugs, dissent and sexual perversion. He has already imagined her a nymphomaniac and checked his penis for welts or boils. Watching her patiently and politely working with the general's wife, she seems quite different from the one woman he met who actually probably was a true nymphomaniac, someone who had volunteered to go 'on the block' at the Johnsonville Rugby Club on more than one occasion, the infamous Tonya Hawkins. His curiosity in her wasn't returned one quiet night at a friend's house. She looked through him with eyes so passive and expressionless they seemed drugged; the high painted eyebrows registered continual incongruous surprise. Miss Kurosawa has long natural eyebrows. Her blue hair and height mark her out. She doesn't walk pigeon-toed and speak inanities in a helium voice to please Japanese men. Mind you, at twenty-five, he thinks, she's a little too old for that. He listens to her interact with the general's wife. Although she inhabits the space of continual playful astonishment that polite conversation sometimes requires, uses the correct honorifics liberally, and defers and listens, something is missing. He doesn't know what. Is it that she sees herself as the older woman's equal? Arrogance, maybe, is her fault. Maybe she's in New Zealand to have that flaw corrected. Or she's a spy and feels superior to a housewife, even one married to a general. When the class ends she doesn't straggle, and is out the door before several others. Why me? he thinks. He looks through the Transport section in the textbook. The lesson for tomorrow, 'Talking about cars', will give him ample opportunity to say, 'My car has broken down,' and cancel tomorrow night's meeting.

That night, he rings Marty. Marty, Bill and three other guys from the team live in a five-bedroom house in Island Bay. Bill answers and says, 'Chris, practice on Tuesday at five, usual place. Good on ya.'

'I'm after a game on Saturday, Bill.'

'Eh?' He sounds hungover. 'Seriously? Nah, not this week. Most of the boys are off to Christchurch tonight to watch the big game.'

'Ah, yeah. Marty said.'

'Yeah. Heaps of clubs going. Shit weather but they probably won't even notice, eh. Too busy pissing it up.'

'You're not going?'

'Nah, mate. What is it about locks and work? I dunno. You're a bad influence.'

'Speaking of bad influences, how's Wannabe going?' He means Coach Wantanabe, who was decreed the Typhoons' new coach after they won the championship last year. Winning teams always get lumped with Japanese coaches.

'Ah, he's all right. Good on the fitness and knows when to get out of the way. He doesn't want to change things too much in case we start losing. Still weird though; it's like being back at school sometimes. He had a beer the other night and his face went bright red. He saw the funny side.'

'You sound a bit crook, mate.'

'Yeah, I'm pretty shit actually. Look, I'll come and see you next week. I have a proposition to make.' He means that Chris should play rugby.

'All right, mate, I'm curious. Looking forward to it.'

He's a little put out that Bill didn't mention the trip to Christchurch earlier, even though he doesn't want to go. The only reason he knows about it is because Marty wanted his hair cut. He really must get Saturdays off next season. He's losing touch with the boys. And Saturday nights off too, for God's sake, he thinks, so I can meet a woman who won't cost me my life.

At 10 the next morning he's still in bed, listening to the rain, trying to bask in a sensation of relief after confirming in his mind beyond doubt that he won't pick Miss Kurosawa up at 11 pm in the car park by the zoo that night. I'm free, he tells himself. I'm safe. It's unusual for him to stay in bed so long, but the sense of a treat he's striving for continues to elude him. The phone rings and he knows it's Patrick.

'Bro.'

'Hey, Chris, what did you find out?' He speaks English and sounds stressed.

'I saw Endo speaking at the conference. He's conservative, but . . . my main impression is that he's busy. If he did have something to do with it, it was on his own initiative, not an army project. You know what I mean?'

'No.'

'They would have used someone less busy.'

'Right.'

'But the fact he was seeing Chiyo is not 100 percent wholesome. He's the pin-up boy in education. I assume he's married. Some kind of threat of blackmail may get him talking? I dunno—'

'I'll do it.'

'How're you going, Pat?'

'I'm angry, Chris. I've never been so angry. I'm consumed with fucking rage. You know I get angry sometimes, but never like this . . .'

He remembers his brother getting very angry sometimes, like the time when the house Chris and his mother lived in was burnt down. And he was censured for fighting outside the ring a couple of times. 'How's Chiyo?' Chris asks.

'She's avoiding me.'

'Right.'

'The brakes on the Mazda. My mechanic couldn't call it. The car's riddled with rust and the handbrake didn't work anyway. It wasn't obvious. He said someone could have expanded some rust damage.'

'What'd Doober say?'

'He said he doesn't know anything. I have reason to believe him.'

'What reason?'

'I hurt him, Chris. And he talked.'

'Hurt him? What did you do?'

Patrick sighs in reply and although Chris is shocked by the act of violence his brother considers unspeakable, he feels a thrill of excitement and pride. 'Was Jock there?'

'The little guy? The skinhead?'

'Yeah.'

'He took off.'

Chris has a sense of what a ferocious opponent his brother would make in the ring. But his anger is dangerous. He won't presume to tell his brother to calm down, so he says, 'I'm angry too, Patrick. It got me thrown in the cells.'

'Okay. Good advice. Take it easy. I'm trying, believe me. Look, could you check out those lunatics the Lord's Angels for me?'

When Patrick hangs up, Chris takes Doober's card from his wallet, which has the address of the Lord's Angels scrawled on the back. On an impulse, he rings Doober's office number. No one answers. He's about to get the operator to put him through to the hospital when he decides to run up Mount Victoria instead. But the weather's filthy, a freezing southerly with bursts of icy rain, and he only gets halfway up before he turns back. The weather will ruin the big game in Christchurch, he thinks. It'll be a mudbath. The trip down on the ferry would have been miserable too. Everyone will have been too seasick to drink and fight. They would have tried, though; made a valiant effort. He grins at the thought, and feels he's missing out.

Showered back to warmth and mellowed by endorphins, he turns on the radio and hears the impossible news that the Wellington to Lyttelton Ferry has disappeared. It did not reach port and is feared lost. No distress signal was received, which may be due to storm damage sustained by the Mount Kaukau radio transmitter. The search is hampered by the bad weather. He can't believe what he's hearing. He sees his teammates clinging to wreckage in the freezing ocean, waiting in vain for rescue. It can't be true. He rings Marty's house but no one answers. He tries five more numbers, urging someone to pick up. *Please pick up, please pick up.* But they all ring and ring with no answer.

# Chapter 11: Mutiny:

# The Typhoons set sail

Marty huddles with ten of his Typhoon teammates among the more than seven hundred rugby players in the ferry terminal, waiting in the big, cold, concrete-and-tin barn for the late sailing. Their breath steams. Their murmur, broken by the occasional exuberant shout, sounds like a crowd before kick-off. Marty notes that each team has a different way of dealing with the tension and excitement. The Typhoons, the Wellington Senior A champions, are tight and focused, all moving on the spot but maintaining their silent huddle as they warm themselves and shake off their anxiety before performing their crucial role in the coming hours. Some of the other teams, B and C grade in particular, are all over the place, peeling off shouts into the echoing space, sparring, probably drinking. Unbelievably, the sweet and heavy scent of marijuana drifts over. It's like sparking up before playing the final—madness. The Typhoons tersely share their disbelief.

The nerves are familiar, like those they experienced before the final at Athletic Park last season, a game played in similarly appalling weather, although in daylight. Marty didn't sleep the night before that either. The fake Russian uniform beneath his clothes feels a bit like a rugby jersey, as if he'll take off his warm jacket and run onto the field in it. He would share this thought with his circle of mates, puffing and blowing, pale from more than just the cold in the unheated terminal, but only three of them wear the hidden uniforms. Many of the boys don't know about them; they have different jobs and will separate into smaller units on board. This sense of apartness from his mates doesn't sit well with him. It reminds him of his girlfriend whom he will never see again, and how he wasn't allowed to tell her anything, not even hint at it. Not telling his parents made sense, but not telling Claire felt dishonest. Some of the guys pulled out on account of their girlfriends: Jonno, Baz, Kev. Kev has kids already. But Ron is married, and he's coming. Marty notes that Ron's beanie is pulled low. Did he tell his wife?

Claire comes to mind again, his 'good egg'—their pet name for each other. Five months together, most of it not seriously . . . something he likes a lot about her. Perhaps a girl in Australia will call him her good egg. He feels he has betrayed Claire by not telling her anything, by disappearing without saying goodbye. But Brian was particularly firm on that point, particularly vehement that girlfriends and mothers must not be told. Many of the boys don't have fathers to tell, Marty thinks, which was probably why Brian didn't mention them. Brian returns and stands at the centre of the circle, small and neat, like a flame protected from the wind.

'It's just like a big game, boys,' he tells them. 'Once the whistle blows you'll be fine. We're not up against other Kiwis this time, we're together fighting the enemy.'

Hail bangs on the tin roof like machine-gun fire. A burst of laughter sounds hollow and forced. Marty marked the incumbent All Black in last year's final and feared humiliation and failure, but not death at sea as well. From the other side of the terminal comes a manic shout; a chant fails miserably to take.

'Those drunks won't be any good tonight, or tomorrow,' Brian tells them.

Marty wishes for a shot of something to calm his nerves.

'Here, this'll warm you up,' says Brian, as he pulls out a hip flask. Eleven men look hungrily at it. Brian produces a second flask and passes it the other way. He doesn't take any himself. He is an old man good with a knife, still quick and dangerous and full of hate for the Japanese. Marty thinks of him again as a still candle flame, holding its lines impeccably.

It's not long before the team is huddled together, arm in arm, exactly as they would before a game, something they would have been embarrassed to do before the vodka. Marty feels the group power, the unity, the bond of trust. They won the final in the hail. He outplayed the All Black Open-Side Flanker. They are the reigning champions. They will win.

On board the ferry, the forwards stand outside near the stern, out of the worst of the wind. The illuminated flags of Japan, the red and rising suns, stretch and turn imperiously, high on their masts. Below them, poorly lit, is the bastard New Hokkaido flag.

Plate scowls. 'Those red fuckin' suns are coming down.'

Marty shakes Plate's hand and slaps his shoulder in a show of confidence. The others follow his lead, silently pledging themselves again to each other and the task ahead. They don't look up again, but watch the trucks file into the boat, lights blazing. Each one, Marty knows, contains a tank filled to the brim with diesel, and some with guns in metal tubes welded to their chassis. He tries to feel something for

Wellington, but only Japanese lights burn this late. For a moment he feels vindicated, righteous and fearless. Until Stew slaps his shoulder and points out a woman in a heavy coat standing alone on the dock, looking up at the ship. For a second he thinks it's Claire. Or hopes it is. Then he can't look at her, and feels for the player who has to deal with this protracted, silent reproach. It's too much.

'Fuck, mate,' says Tunny, his voice thick with emotion. 'That's hardcore.'

'True.'

'Mate . . .'

'Someone blabbed,' says Plate, the acting captain in Bill's absence. 'Loose lips sink ships.'

This judgement, although somewhat harsh in Marty's opinion, stops further comment, and he is glad that Plate, the Number Eight, is also secretly wearing a Russian uniform. The guy is someone you want on your side in a fight.

He's grateful for the distraction when the Hooker takes a section of hacksaw blade from his shoe and discreetly gets to work on a rail. The pack surrounds and hides him. No one says much. Someone wonders what the backs are doing. 'Probably going over in first class,' Marty replies, and gets a valuable laugh. As the Hooker moves to the next rail, Marty has the sensation of a satisfying first contact after kick-off. He thinks they can do it. The fear has gone and it's all about rhythm, accuracy and teamwork. Bogie will saw off the other ends once the boat clears the heads and the rails will become weapons.

But when the ferry is underway and he and the other loosies, Tunny and Plate, are in the toilet stripping down to their fake Russian uniforms, he feels weak with fear, almost sick, far worse than he did before the final. Tunny is very pale, having vomited, as he often does, before a big game. The uniforms look wrong: too thin, too cheap, too light a shade of green. Even on Plate it looks wrong.

'Good,' says Brian. 'You look the part. You'll get us in.'

He lifts the lid off a cistern and fishes out a bottle of vodka. After wiping it with a paper towel he hands it to Marty, who notes the steadiness of Brian's hand.

'If they look blank at you through the door, wave this at them.'

The ship begins to roll and pitch. Things are moving fast.

'It's water, not vodka,' Brian adds.

One knock, then two short ones. Brian cracks the door and grins. A tall man Brian's age comes in and shakes his hand.

'This is Jimmy, the other shooter,' Brian tells the three loose forwards.

Marty likes the look of the rangy newcomer. He's dressed all in black and, though sixty-odd, is still broad and powerful. Jimmy reaches into a shoulder holster hidden beneath his jacket and hands Brian a machine pistol and a handful of magazines.

'This is a Russian Stechkin machine pistol,' says Jimmy. 'You've probably seen them with the butt attached. Watch closely, boys, because you'll be picking one up in the bar from a Russian who doesn't need it anymore. This is the safety catch. On, off. You have nineteen shots in a magazine. This is how you remove it when it's empty. This is how you put a new one in. Set it here to fire single shots, like this. You'll lose a magazine in a couple of seconds otherwise. Mainly, this is the fucking trigger.'

They're in the blasting night on the rolling, pitching deck in their thin green uniforms, the three of them. His newly shaved head is cold. He feels naked. Ahead is the heavy little sea-door, the entrance to the bar for off-duty soldiers. Its window is a little square of light. *It's really happening.* Marty's heart thuds in his chest, yet he feels disembodied, as if the little door is coming to him. It falls to him, the number seven, to try the door handle. He reaches out. He is the whistle, the booted ball, the first roar of the crowd. The door opens easily at his touch. He enters the cabin, his teammates behind him. A dozen Russians, smiling, smoking and drinking. He's on the carpet, floored by a blow between his shoulders. *I'm shot. Am I shot?* Rapid gunfire; an invisible dragon lashes the room, curses, flailing, falling. It's over and he's unharmed. Tunny and Plate are okay. The cabin is full of corpses, men with the life wrenched out of them. Brian fusses about the rolling cabin, pushing bodies, looking for something. He takes a dead man's pistol and crosses smartly to the other side of the cabin and fires into the back of a Russian head. There had been a gurgling sound that Marty wasn't aware of until it stopped. Brian stands over another body and shoots.

'Okay, Brian,' says Jimmy, and he waves in the front row from outside. There is much handshaking and shoulder slapping.

Brian fires again. His voice is high-pitched. 'We don't want any nasty surprises.'

'Take a gun, boys,' Jimmy tells the loosies. 'You'll feel a lot better armed.'

Marty is aware that the heavy machine pistol in his hand didn't do its previous owner any good. The cabin is suddenly full of jubilant players. Brian fires again.

'*Jesus*, Brian.'

'He was alive, Jimmy!'

'Here, mate.' Jimmy takes the pistol from Marty and swiftly checks the magazine. Marty likes Jimmy, who was clearly a lock in his day. His sense of calm and strength remind him of Chris. 'Just point and shoot,' Jimmy says. 'I've taken the safety off. Don't worry about reloading. You blokes have got sixty shots between you now. More than enough for the next phase.'

'Da, comrades,' says Marty in a Russian accent. 'Da, da, da.'

Tunny giggles. 'Marty, for fuck's sake, hit the deck next time.'

'Eh?'

'I had to bring you down, bro.'

Marty puts a hand on Tunny's shoulder. 'You're shitting me.' Tunny's eyes are gleaming. 'Was that you that tackled me?'

Everyone laughs, except the dead men.

'You did good, man,' says Tunny, 'but you stood there like you wanted someone to buy you a drink.'

More laughter.

Plate slaps Marty's back. 'Nah, full credit to you, bro. That took nuts.'

'You guys have an understanding,' says Jimmy. 'That's why we chose you. Having said that, no one was going to buy you a drink, Number Seven. You can hit the deck straight away next time.'

Brian, separated from the general jubilation, is crouched over a dead young man, blond and Kiwi-like, with his finger at the man's throat as if hoping for a pulse. His hand jerks back, revealing a red knife. Blood pools on the green lino.

'Brian, *for fuck's sake*—'

Almost furtively, Brian cuts another throat. Then he wipes his blade clean on the dead man's uniform and springs for the door.

'Let's go,' he cries in a high-pitched voice. 'Same again on the bridge, lads, and we're on our way to Australia.'

'Hang on,' says Jimmy, 'that's not the plan.'

'Come on! We're still heading south. We need to be going northwest.'

'Wait!' Jimmy runs out of the cabin after Brian. The

Typhoons loosies follow, under the impression they are rushing to haul Brian in, but as soon as they hit the black night air, their backs are slapped and they slow as players part for them like a guard of honour. Marty has the sensation of riding a wave as they make their way in darkness over the rolling deck, of being swept by an irresistible force. They are the spearhead flying to the heart of the enemy. The guards are not at their usual posts. The way has been cleared for them. In a moment they are in the Tourist Section, where he has never dared set foot before, surging up the plushly carpeted corridor with its polished wood.

# Chapter 12:

# Ice and fire

Miss Kurosawa's absence from the 5 pm class on Friday settles the issue of their meeting that night once and for all. There's no way it will happen. He just needs to apologise next week, say something came up, and it's over. Spectacular while it lasted, but . . . He works late, planning lessons in the staffroom. The missing ferry is commented on. He wonders if he should get drunk. A teacher says fifty Japanese crew and soldiers were on board, along with the eight hundred passengers, numbers that the media have been cagey about. The teachers talk about how it was mainly rugby players travelling south for the big match, how family groups avoid those late sailings when Wellington plays in Christchurch, given the reputation for barbaric behaviour. After the teachers have voiced their disapproval the conversation ends. But they know something else, he can tell. The story's too big and they're working a little too scrupulously for a Friday night. The real conversation will begin when he leaves.

He decides to test his hypothesis by asking the deputy principal if he can leave early. Before he can even open his mouth he is waved away. Something's definitely up. He packs his briefcase, bows to the room and excuses himself. In return he's thanked for his work in a distracted way by the younger staff members. After sitting in a cubicle in the men's bathroom for ten minutes he returns to the staffroom on the pretext of forgetting a textbook and hears the buzz of animated conversation.

He was right. From his vantage point near the door at the front of the staffroom, close to where the speakers are gathered at the principal's desk, it quickly becomes clear to him that they don't know much for certain. What they do know is that the radio transmitter at Mount Kaukau was sabotaged rather than storm-damaged on the night the ferry disappeared. So no distress call could be sent in a mutiny, he thinks. It was planned. *They'll be heading for Australia.* He turns away, holding his breath, and walks quickly and quietly down the corridor. For a couple of seconds his back feels acutely exposed and a shout from a teacher imminent. He makes the door and bursts outside into the freezing gale. As he plunges down the steps a general clatter of iron and metal announces the arrival of hail. A cry of joy or anger comes with it as he runs across the road to the sanctuary of Paddy's.

The fire near the entrance is piled high and radiates warmth. They might be safe, he thinks. Safe on board, heading for Australia. This is the more measured end of the bar, where couples and older people come to have a quiet drink. In a mood for happy reflection he takes an empty table near the window, not too far from the fire, and lays his coat over the chair.

'Bad night to be at sea,' the barman says as he pours Chris a pint of Asahi Gold.

'I just heard,' Chris replies, leaning forward and lowering his voice, 'that the radio transmitter was sabotaged.'

The barman raises his eyebrows.

'Maybe that's why the crew was unable to send a distress call.'

'Source?'

'Just overheard it.'

'On me, mate.'

'Cheers.'

Taking his free beer and the barman's approval to his table by the window, he sits and watches hail pop in the street. He's very happy, yet it's a bittersweet happiness at the same time, because he knows he won't see Marty or his teammates ever again. If not drowned, they're still gone; for him it's nearly the same loss in practical terms. It occurs to him that even if they have taken control of the vessel, it's still a long way to Australia, and the air force will have the option of sinking the ferry when the weather clears. Or they may even be able to intercept it with a destroyer. That would be the preferred option for the IJA: to avoid an international incident by bringing everyone home and locking them up forever. It's another bad outcome, and he reminds himself that his theory of an organised mutiny is just speculation at this stage. Marty's behaviour at their last meeting is further evidence, though. Maybe compelling evidence. Something was up with the haircut and the locks for his mum. I wasn't trusted, he thinks. It hurts.

Two young blond women are blown in by the storm. He watches the barman tell them something, probably the information about the transmitter, as he mixes rum and colas. You could send them over here, mate, for the full story, Chris thinks, growing courageous after one beer on an empty stomach. Drinks in hand, the women head down past the barbecue booths to the raucous end of the pub where the pool tables are. The space is marked off by three-quarters of a wall. They disappear into a cloud of cigarette smoke from which comes the crack of pool balls, laughter, the new

Irish band U2 on the jukebox. He considers following the women, but not seriously, having learned his lesson from the New Zealand Culture evening about the perils of socialising in a suit. On the way back from the toilet he peers inside the smoky section anyway. There are half a dozen slight and pale young Irishmen playing pool, drinking and generally holding court, dressed in green and with Gaelic script on their T-shirts. They're popular with Kiwi women. One time Marty put on a green T-shirt and an Irish accent in the hope of scoring but his size and robust colour didn't indicate generational malnutrition and gave him away immediately. His cries of protest—'Oim big because oi grew up on a faarm!'—didn't wash. Once, an Irishman told Chris: 'The English are fookin' tiny, man!' Irish pubs are popular in Wellington because of Ireland's neutrality in World War II and their ongoing friendly relations, which includes the Irish on-selling New Zealand beef and lamb to Great Britain as 'Irish Produce'. Chris likes the Irish. They're a good source of information about Great Britain and the US. They don't know much about Soviet Europe though, so it will be useless asking them about the Paris riots. He thanks the barman and heads for home. The hail is sporadic now. The odd bang is either the arrival of the last high-frozen stones, or terrestrial objects picked up by the gale and brought to a sudden stop. It's been only a week since, in the house on Mount Victoria, he heard about Sarah's murder. He wonders if the players' meeting he was excluded from was about the mutiny.

His apartment is cold. He lights the kerosene heater by the sliding door and cracks it open for ventilation. The gale sucks and whistles. The animated clatter of a tin can comes loudly from the ground below. He closes the door, puts out the heater and changes into his wool jersey and heavy leather jacket. On impulse he takes a blanket with him.

He has a very good car for a young New Zealander: a

1980 Toyota Corolla sedan with a 2.8-litre engine. He's particularly fond of the stereo, an AM/FM radio and cassette player with 30-watt amp and speakers back and front. It's been a while since he's driven, and despite the filthy weather he enjoys it. The heater soon warms him up. He feels cocooned. A violent squall of rain comes in and he turns the wipers to maximum. No problem. There are few cars about. Those he sees on the way to Island Bay crawl through ponds on the road; lights puddle, slip and fracture across his windscreen.

He stops outside Bill and Marty's dark house in Derwent Street. There is a chance that Bill might be in, he thinks, lying low. The old Datsun van the guys share is in the drive. Given that houses where rugby players reside are occasionally raided by the army, he would normally park down the street to prevent his car's possible seizure, but it's 10 pm and the night is rotten. He has to push the car door open, fight the wind to get out. The sea roars and its pungency floods over him. A freezing battering ram. The weather is exhilaratingly bad. The gale slams the car door shut. Grabbed and buffeted, he runs up the side of the house. Suddenly in shelter, he tries the back door. It opens. He finds the light switch in the kitchen and a mouse bolts under the fridge, scritching its claws on the lino. 'Bill? Bill? It's Chris.' He half expects to see a possum in the lounge. Instead he finds surprising neatness. The coffee table, a slab of macrocarpa with eighty-seven or eighty-eight rings, is clear of bottles and cans. Even the ashtray is empty. It's cold. 'Bill?' He knocks on Bill's door. 'It's Chris. I have a spliff.' He has a strong sense he shouldn't be there.

He drives around the south coast, in the teeth of the storm, in awe of the sea's fury as it detonates and rushes over the rocky shore. His headlights seem to freeze white foam in midair after the thump of heavy impact. As he enters

Breaker Bay a man in a red-and-black bush shirt steps out onto the road waving his arms. Unshaven, haggard, there is desperation in him. Chris goes around him and accelerates away. The colony survives solely on the food they grow in their gardens and catch in the sea. The object is to have nothing to do with the occupying forces, which includes their electricity, and it's a bitter place in winter.

A two-storeyed wooden house is on fire across the cove, reflecting redly on the white blanket of surf over black seawater. The top right corner is engulfed. Chris stops and winds down his window. A tongue of flame leaps into the sky and sends a shower of sparks in a low, flat trajectory into the dark hillside behind. A long crackling gust makes the flames appear to falter. Darkness creeps back as the gust continues. Figures out front on the grass hold up their hands. The wind stalls, and flames and sparks erupt skyward, brighter than before, in a muscular release.

He thinks of his boyhood home, the boarding house in Newtown his mother ran, how he came home from school, noticing first the flowing gutters at the bottom of Constable Street on a sunny day, then the smell before he turned into Owen Street, a strange patch of smoky mist over the rooftops, then the crowd of strangers, the daytime pulse of fire sirens, the criss-cross of flat hoses. It's my house, he told a fireman. The man took his hand and looked around. Uncertain, he took Chris down the driveway. The back half of the house was smoky, steamy, stinky; a wreckage. The roof had collapsed and twisted. The oven was a black stub, the only thing still standing. Firemen in heavy gear were crunching in their boots, looking for something in the charred and soaking remains. It was still warm; things trickled and popped. His mother appeared from nowhere and grabbed him and nearly crushed the breath out of him. She smelled of smoke. Her body heaved with sobs.

He puts the car into gear. No one in front of the burning house tries to stop him as he passes. There is a phonebox at the Seatoun shops. It works, and he calls 111. The operator tells him that the fire service is already on its way. She's a Kiwi, so it might be true. He continues around the peninsula. Scorching Bay is still windy, but nothing like the south coast. He remembers the boarding house. It was a gift from Patrick, a place to live and earn money at a time when money was hard to come by for solo mothers. But because his mother owned it freehold, she ran it more like a charity than a business, according to Patrick. He would tell Chris about it on the phone from Japan. Eventually Chris would pass the phone to his mother. During his brother's calls, she would sometimes put the phone down and light a cigarette and Patrick would keep scolding her from Japan and never notice.

Money was not the real source of tension in the house though; that revolved around an ethnic Chinese woman, Katrina, whom his mother was hiding. Ethnic Chinese were thought to harbour anti-Japanese sentiment and were routinely executed in the first years of the occupation. The entire Auckland population was rounded up and shot in 1943. It had been inexplicable to most New Zealanders, who thought Chinese and Japanese were basically the same people. Chris's mother had met Katrina through a mutual friend who had hidden her for a decade in her attic. Katrina would come down at night and babysit and cook for the family. A fine arrangement, until the couple separated and sold the house.

Katrina was about forty-five, the same age as Chris's mother, when she moved into the boarding house. She stayed in her room and sewed and knitted. She made Chris elaborate jerseys. Her room smelled funny and so did the garments she made until they were washed. She ate all her meals in her room and used a chamber pot as well. Sometimes, when the other boarders were out, she would cook a big Chinese meal using Japanese ingredients like ginger, soy sauce, noodles, fish and rice. She spoke English with an accent like a Japanese as well. Two of the other boarders weren't sympathetic. They used Katrina as an excuse not to pay rent. 'If she doesn't pay,' said old Mr Parsons from the first war, 'why should I?' He used to refer to her as a Jap and a Yellow Devil. He talked about her a lot. Chris's mother explained to Chris that she couldn't kick Mr Parsons out because he would go to the police. The other boarder who took exception to Katrina was a woman of about thirty-five, a typist named Nadine, who also refused to pay rent. She wanted Katrina's room as well. She said that the windows in Katrina's room were wasted because the curtains were always drawn. Why couldn't Katrina have her smaller, windowless room? Chris's mother would tell her that Katrina needed a larger room because she lived in it all day every day. Nadine kept complaining to old Mr Parsons about it. It was all they ever talked about as far as Chris could tell. And then Patrick would ring from Japan about the finances and his mother would put the phone down and light a cigarette. When Chris came home from school one day, Katrina was gone. His mum told him she'd gone to a safer place. One of his most vivid memories of that time is Nadine beginning to move her stuff into Katrina's room and his mother throwing it out onto the street. He'd been surprised by her strength and fury. There was a lot of yelling, and bad language even. Nadine left in tears, taking her few possessions. But his mother's fury had not abated. When she began throwing Mr Parsons' stuff onto the street as well, he'd joined in and helped. A few days later the fire happened.

Past Karaka Bay, on the north side of the peninsula, it

110

is much calmer. He parks in a nook of stone at Shelly Bay, gets out of the car and lights a cigarette. Out in the open harbour, spray is lifting off the white caps, but in the bay itself, close to shore, the black water over the fish farms is merely ruffled. Lights from the large houses on the hill break and shimmer. It's an affluent neighbourhood, mainly Maori, and supported by these fish farms and other cooperative fishing ventures. He likes the neighbourhood and keeps an eye on real-estate prices. Anywhere from here around to Maupuia in an elevated north-facing house would be great if he could afford it. It strikes him as infinitely preferable to the colony at Breaker Bay and a concrete demonstration of the advantages of working constructively with the occupation forces. He thinks of Marty and his teammates and the options they have chosen: escape, or death. Either way they're gone. They've left him. There's a disagreeable hiss in the pines; five minutes is long enough to get cold. He gets back in the car.

People are dying and disappearing on him. He wishes he had someone to hold on to. Hitomi Kurosawa is definitely someone. It's nearly 11 pm when he pulls into the small car park in front of the zoo. The trees surrounding it flex and bluster in the wind. He turns off the engine and headlights and unlocks the back doors. Maybe police or soldiers will wrench it open, he thinks. The dark thrashing trees, the feeling of confinement in the small enclosed car park, make it seem almost inevitable. I'm being set up for public humiliation, he thinks. It's a morality lesson for the public, the fall of the Night Train and his family, orchestrated by the Imperial Japanese Army. It's a trap. He reaches for the ignition just as the back door opens.

# Chapter 13: Mutiny:

## Brian takes it to the bridge

Marty is grateful for the carpet that muffles their footsteps as they trot down the corridor of the tourist section. They've all been briefed on how crucial the advantage of surprise is. Some wooden doors are open, revealing empty cabins, tidy and luxurious. They look unused. Then there's a cabin strewn with sheets and blankets and littered with rice crackers. Brian yells, 'Out of the way!' and ahead Marty sees a crowd of yellow-and-black-clad players huddled inside a doorway. It takes a moment to sink in that he is not actually in the vanguard. Jimmy is impassive. If Plate and Tunny are surprised they give nothing away. Brian pushes through the crowd and wrenches open the door at the end of the corridor.

'Wait!' someone yells. When Jimmy charges after him, Marty follows with Tunny and Plate, and they find themselves at the bottom of a steep flight of steps leading up to the bridge. The steel door at the top is shut. The vibration of the ship's engine becomes apparent. At the foot of the steps two older men crouch over plastic explosives and a detonator; on each wall stand two players with machine pistols and grenades, evidently taken from Japanese guards. They are bracing themselves against the ship's movement. Marty sees the plan: to blow the door open.

Brian yells in his high-pitched voice: 'Have you tried the door?'

The men with the explosives look up and, seeming to recognise him, shake their heads wordlessly. It's very quiet.

'Give me that!' Brian takes a couple of grenades from a player, and before anyone can say anything he springs up the stairs, opens the door a fraction, pulls the pin from a grenade, tosses it inside and shuts the door. *Whump.* He's inside and there's a long burst of gunfire. Jimmy, suddenly at the head of the steps, leaps through the smoky doorway. There's another burst. Standing with the others around the bottom of the steps, Marty is temporarily frozen. Acrid smoke blows down in a rush of cold air. A single shot rings out. Then another. Jimmy appears in the doorway.

'The bridge is ours!'

Another shot.

The bridge is dark and cold. There are four dead sailors. Half the glass has been blown out, along with most of the lights, and rain rides the torrent of cold air coming in. Brian lifts a head by the hair and cuts its throat—the captain's, judging by his ornate uniform. Still the engine runs and the bow pitches into the waves. Brian wipes clean his blade and steps smartly to avoid the growing puddle of blood.

'Victory!' Marty yells hoarsely at Brian.

Plate drops a long and powerful arm across Marty's chest, the same arm of restraint he feels when he's being niggled inside their own twenty-two during a close match. Players race up the stairs and pile in behind them, shouting triumphantly.

'Out, out,' Jimmy shouts into the commotion.

A shot brings silence. The wind howls and the ocean explodes over the bow. Brian has fired into the air this time, out into the night.

'We have to turn the ship around,' Jimmy says. 'Everybody out except the bridge crew. Go and get something to board up these windows. A couple of tables might do the trick. See if you can dig up a rivet gun. And take these bodies with you. Chuck 'em over the side.'

Being among the last of the players left on the bridge, they have to lug a bloody corpse away. Jimmy wraps a jacket around the captain's cut throat but his head hinges back when lifted by the arms and legs, and he leaks an alarming amount of blood. Brian has disappeared.

'Turn him over,' Jimmy tells them.

'Nice work, Brian,' Marty mutters.

'You three,' Jimmy says. 'After you've dumped this joker, follow Brian down to the Security Centre. We're keen to capture hostages if possible.'

'Got you,' Plate says.

The other major phase of the operation is the capture of the ship's Security Centre. That's Plan A. Plan B is to contain and isolate the fifty or so well-armed soldiers who man it, and prevent them leaving it to recapture the bridge. Heavy guns smuggled in on the trucks are being used for this part of the operation.

As soon as the loosies have dumped the dead captain overboard, a player yells out, 'Russkies!' It's fortunate he's unarmed.

'We're not fuckin' Russians, you dumb-arse!' Plate shouts.

The three of them immediately remove their green jackets and throw them away.

'I'm cold.'

'We've gotta get warm.'

They head for the toilet where their clothes are stashed.

Marty remembers the question he asked himself as he stuffed his clothes away under the sink: whether he'd be back for them. A surge of pure excitement and optimism goes through him as he puts his foot into his jeans. The ship lurches, and he goes flying. Plate and Tunny also go over but not as spectacularly.

'Shit. You okay, bro?'

The ship's turning, a thrilling sensation, but also terrifying as it broadsides the oncoming weather. They stay on the toilet floor as the rolling and pitching intensifies. The door flies open and curses go up in the nearby lounge area. The engine announces itself by cutting out. Cold fear clutches Marty's heart. The ship slams down and rolls appallingly, and after a few very long seconds, the engine resumes. A couple more gasp-inducing rolls and the storm is behind them, driving them on.

'Woohoo!'

'Australia, here we come!'

'You fuckin' beauty!'

'A quick drink before we catch up with Brian, lads? Quick being the key word.'

'Hang on,' says Plate.

'We've earned it,' says Tunny.

'A *very* quick drink,' says Plate. 'Down the hatch and off.'

But the bar they cleared and have a right to is surrounded and packed full. They manage to push through the crowd but there is no chance of squeezing inside. Body heat and the smell of vomit emanate from the cabin, and the loud babble of voices is punctuated by shouts and war cries. The happy faces they glimpse are flushed.

'Into the vodka, lucky bastards.'

'Hey,' comes a cry from behind, 'it's the Russians.'

Tunny accepts a half-full bottle of vodka and takes a swig.

'Fair play to youse fullas.'

Marty's shoulder is slapped. The eyes of the strangers upon him, triumphant and bleary with drink, are also strangely shy. Aware of the pistol on his hip, he takes a shot of vodka. They want him to say something.

'We're on our way, boys. This time tomorrow night we'll be free.'

'I'll drink to that,' says Plate, taking a mighty gulp from the bottle.

The vodka is welcome, but standing outside on the rolling deck with strangers is not what Marty had imagined. And the toast feels hollow: they will be out of New Zealand's 300-kilometre economic zone by mid-morning but it will take another forty-eight hours to get even halfway to Australia, and the Japanese navy is large and quick and aircraft carriers are based in Auckland. He feels they should get back to work, but Jimmy's request to rein Brian in seems impossible, and it's Plate's call anyway, being captain. The man might half listen to Jimmy during his blood-frenzy, but really . . . Marty doesn't want to put himself in the way of that unstoppable force, that bloodlust. The bottle comes around and he takes another hit.

'Brian's a hard case,' he offers.

They hear the question in his voice and listen. The ship is heading northwest to Australia because of him.

'Fuckin' legend.'

'Fearsome soldier.'

The tourists on board flash into his mind, the defenceless women and children huddled somewhere. He says to Plate and Tunny, 'The rest of the boys must be taking the Security Centre. We should get down there.'

'Mmmm.'

'Being armed and everything.'

'Let's go,' says Plate.

# Chapter 14:

# Alone with Miss Kurosawa

It's Miss Kurosawa at the car door, not a platoon of soldiers. 'I think I heard an escaped tiger!' she says as she climbs in.

His heart is still pounding. To convey a sense of relaxation he leans against his door and places one foot on the passenger seat and the other in the foot-well below. His left hand rests on the back of the passenger's seat, close to her. 'You're safe now, Miss Kurosawa,' he says.

Her face flashes in its signature way, but this time the smile lingers. 'Call me Hitomi,' she says, 'and thank you for coming.'

'I wanted to see you.'

She nods. 'Did you bring a blanket?'

'I did. On the floor there.'

'Oh good.'

He looks out the passenger window, continuing his project of looking relaxed while she covers herself with the blanket. She's rummaging. If she takes her clothes off, he thinks, I'm leaving. It's a set-up.

She's waiting for him when he turns back, transformed by a blond wig and blue-tinted sunglasses. The wig has a low straight fringe and falls to her shoulders. Her full lips curve into a smile. Her skin is creamy and flawless, tight over her cheekbones. He looks again and notices the large jersey with a loose collar and the lumberjack shirt beneath it, done up to the top button: her idea of Kiwi women's fashion. It's weird under the expensive glossy wig.

'How do I look?' she asks.

He undoes her top button, undoes the second and third, exposing the fine bones of her clavicle traced by the run of a fine gold chain. He looks again at the transforming blond hair, her lips, and the glimpse of décolletage. 'Perfect,' he says.

'I'm your Kiwi girlfriend, eh?' she says in English.

She looks so exotic, otherworldly even, that the thought of her being a convincing Kiwi makes him laugh. 'From a distance.'

'Shall we go?'

'This is as good a spot as any. It's dark, I mean. Not visible from the road.'

'Let's look at the storm.'

He didn't expect this. An odd request from this picture of poised android perfection.

'Yes,' he says in Japanese. He turns around and starts the car.

She claps. 'Exciting.'

'I wonder if you should get in the front? That's what Kiwi girlfriends do.'

'Yes,' she says in Japanese. When she's next to him in the front seat, the old jersey is revealed in its full shapeless glory. She looks strange. But whatever she looks like, it's not Japanese. He turns on the lights. As he puts the car in gear he sees that she has presented her face to him for a kiss, a 'hello, dear' type kiss, and he realises she is terribly needy and obsessive. 'Mmmm?' She raises her eyebrows.

She wants a kiss, all right, and he can't ignore her now. Her beseeching android head is almost comical in its desperation. 'Kiss please, honey,' she says, and now he gets it. She *is* being comical, playing the old and familiar girlfriend. He plants a dutiful kiss and heads up over the hill for the south coast, savouring the finish of the kiss on his lips. He's happy, glad he picked her up now. They click. She's genuine, and looks hot in the wig. 'Let's look at the storm' is not what the IJA would want her to say if catching them having sex was their object. He has a lot to ask her but doesn't know where to begin. The ferry, he decides, as they crest the hill and feel the force of the wind. A squall sets in as they descend to Lyall Bay. The wipers are on maximum and he slows to a crawl. Her face is illuminated by the headlights of an oncoming car. He stops to let the car pass and the light tracks slowly over her, dimmed and dappled by the rain on the windscreen. She was visible to the other driver. It's exciting. He wonders if she feels it too. At Lyall Bay he turns right and within seconds the lights are behind them and they are burrowing into darkness with the car's headlights. Ghostly surf rears up and spray lashes the window. 'Oh,' she says. He turns off the road, seemingly into the sea, and she cries out again. They are in a pitch black car park below the road, where stoners and couples come, right on the rocky shore. He turns the lights off and she claps. 'Good spot.' Rain drums on the roof and the windscreen.

'I can't run the heater in case the battery goes flat. Let's get under the blanket in the back seat.'

'Yes.'

They get out and she cries, 'Oh, my wig!' A brief struggle with the gale ensues and she manages to hold on to it. The air is raw. He catches a glimpse of white boiling surf rushing over jagged rocks before he ducks into the back seat, wet from only a second or two in the rain. Hitomi struggles to pull the door open. He pushes it out and she climbs in with a burst of rain. 'Oh!' The wig is lopsided and they laugh.

'Quick, get under the blanket.'

She comes close and he puts his arm around her. Easy, he thinks. She wriggles a bit closer, a clear signal. He moves to kiss her and she responds. She's into it, he thinks. Great.

'I bought these jeans at a kids' shop,' she tells him in English as she pulls them back on. 'And they're still a bit loose. A size ten is way too big. Ha.'

'Did you know that I'm the brother of Patrick Ipswitch, the Night Train, the sumo champion?'

'No!'

'Yes. He's ten years older than me.'

'Oh!' Her smile flashes. 'I used to watch the Night Train all the time in Japan. He was my favourite favourite. I wanted a poster of him, a really big one from the sports shop. I had it picked out and everything, but my father said no.'

'Because the Night Train was a Kiwi?'

'No, because I was a young lady.' She laughs for the first time since he's known her, a warm, full-bodied sound, quite unlike the fashionable high-pitched giggle of female Japanese teachers and students, and she makes no attempt to hide her mouth with her hand.

'What did you do in Japan?'

'Same as here. Remember?'

He remembers her introduction in class, which he regarded as fiction at the time. 'Sell car parts?'

'Yes, very good.' She claps. 'I make sure the Datsun franchises have all the parts they need. I travel a lot by car and mainly alone. That's unusual, right? Drive around Wellington and the Hutt Valley, as far as Palmerston North. I'm the only travelling rep in the company who's not a man.'

'Not a man?' He laughs. He slides his hand down her flat

stomach. The jeans are loose at the top, the belt untied, and his hand has easy passage further down.

'Huh.' She leans back and slides her bum forward. He undoes the buttons and feels how wet she is through her underwear. 'You talk to in-house mechanics and people like that?'

'Yeah, their bosses. The head mechanic sometimes. Ha ha. Important guy.'

'Why me?' he asks, probing deeper.

'Ha.'

'Tell me.'

In reply she pulls her jeans and underwear down to her ankles to give him better access. She's very wet. He starts to finger-fuck her.

'Why me?' he repeats.

'Uh.' She bites her lip.

He slows down. The clitoris is something of a mystery to him but he knows where hers is at least. He tries circling it with his thumb while continuing to finger-fuck her. Her hands stray up under her shirt and she squeezes her own nipples. *Got it*, he thinks. He can't fucking believe how hot she is. She pauses to tug her jeans off. His own pants are still off. He lifts her onto his lap and slides the tip of his cock around teasingly, delaying the condom. 'Do I need one?' he asks her.

'What?'

'A condom.'

'No.'

She straddles him and they are kissing, grinding slowly, when a light flares above on the road.

'Stop.'

In an instant she's off and sitting next to him. They pull up the blanket. The car turns and for a moment the backs of their heads are illuminated: his black buzzcut and her straight blond hair. They see each other in the dazzling slipping light. She's his beautiful exotic partner in crime. The car keeps going. She gets back on top, the best position in the confined space.

'Why me?' he asks.

'You're a man.'

'I have a pulse, you mean?'

'In Japanese?'

'My heart beats so I'm good enough?'

'Huh, I mean, like a man should be, I think. Not a little angry man.'

'I think you're incredible.'

They don't speak for a while.

'Why did you come to New Zealand?'

'To miss the winter.'

So that's what you sound like when you lie, he thinks. The same as you usually do.

'To avoid bad weather,' she adds a moment later. The car shakes with a particularly strong blast of wind. She nods emphatically. 'But I've stayed longer than I planned.'

It's a good enough admission of her Settler status for now. He knows that it's dishonourable, a slur on her character, and won't push the issue. 'You were in Christchurch?'

'Yes.'

'You mentioned a sheep-fucker on the ferry.'

'Ha. Damien was his name. A farmer.'

'How did you meet him?' He is aware that the conversation would flow better in Japanese, but speaking English adds to the thrill of wrongdoing. He's stirring again at the sight of her next to him, a futuristic Japanese woman naked from the waist down under the blanket.

'I got lost on a job. Well, I let myself get lost, yeah? I was in the country and got a flat tyre. I can change a flat tyre very well. Damien stopped to help and saw I was Japanese.

It was a little awkward, but I soon found out he is always a little awkward, with any human. Ha.'

'You visited his farm?'

'Yes. I would stay on weekends. It was quite isolated. A beautiful spot. There was a dam for swimming. I would arrive late and leave late the next day or two days later.'

'What are Japanese men like in a relationship?'

'Huh?'

'I mean, I see a very formal side of my colleagues. I have to leave dinners when the drinking gets serious. I don't really know them, you know?'

She nods.

She's proud of that discipline, he thinks, proud of her nation's men.

'They're all different, right?' That's obvious, her tone says, and the subject is closed.

She wants a smoke. The problem is that they'll have to open a window. He jumps out, bare-bummed, hops in the driver's seat, and turns the car sideways. Back in the seat beside her he opens the window on the sheltered side. He's run out of cigarettes so he takes one of her menthols. The first drag tastes like a minty treat but by the third it tastes weak and unsatisfying. And the wind is too strong. It grabs at them with cold fingers and buffets the smoke away from the window so that it collects around them. He throws his out, half smoked. She follows suit. 'I'm thirsty,' she says.

He drives her to the park at Island Bay. 'There's a public water fountain through that gate,' he tells her. 'Turn right. And hold on to your wig.' When she returns he goes out and drinks his fill. It's very dark. Other nights won't offer the same kind of weather protection. Their chances of being seen will be much higher, no matter where they go.

'I don't have a farm,' he tells her on the way back to the zoo car park. It's near where she lives, in a block of apartments.

'Me either.'

He pulls up under the dark trees. It's a relatively secluded spot. He entertains a coupling on the bonnet, a position which will enable him to move freely. 'Quite summery here,' he says.

'In Japanese?'

'It's like summer here, relatively speaking. We could have a picnic on the blanket.'

She looks out the window.

Too much, he thinks, and tries another angle. 'Maybe we could rent a house up north?'

Her face lights up. She leans forward and kisses him.

'Goodnight, Hitomi,' he says.

'What about the blanket?'

She doesn't like the car bonnet idea, and she's right, it's too exposed. He throws it on the ground in the nearby children's playground, at the top of a rise in a spot sheltered from view and the wind. She removes her jeans and underwear in her usual forthright manner and lies on the blanket. He drops his own trousers and kneels over her.

'What about the licking?' she says.

He manages to conceal his surprise. 'Yes.'

She spreads her legs and he concentrates on her clitoris with his tongue, which works well, judging by her breathing and groans. However, his bare butt's in the air and getting cold. Feeling his own excitement dwindling, he moves up and rubs against her and it slips in. He comes quickly and is surprised at the roar he emits as he pulls out in a spontaneous and inexplicable attempt to prevent a pregnancy. We're crazy, he thinks. He can't pull his pants up quickly enough. He dabs the sperm off her stomach with the blanket. There is also some on her jersey. She's in no hurry to get dressed. Lying there as he impatiently spot-cleans, she runs her hands over her stomach and down the insides of her thighs. Okay, he thinks, I'm not going to make her ask again.

# Chapter 15: Mutiny:

# Waiting for battle

Marty is shocked to hear that the attack on the Security Centre has failed. The plastic explosives didn't detonate and the assault force had to wait at length for one of the three doors to open. A guard was shot and a grenade was thrown in, but the ensuing rush was repelled, with five players being mown down, including two Typhoons. Moments later, the door burst open and six soldiers charged out into the firing line of the machine gun covering the corridor. The soldiers were killed, but three-quarters of the gun's ammunition was spent and one of the gunners was bayoneted.

The stand-off is tense. As many as thirty-five well-armed soldiers are thought to be inside the centre and ready to make a break. The other machine guns don't have good firing lines on the other two exits and are too close to them, so the Typhoons' forward pack is roped into a second ring of defence in a tourist lounge adjacent to the Security Centre. Behind the barricade of tables and couches, only the three loosies are armed. The twenty or so other players that hold the position have only the knives they brought on board or found in the ship's kitchen. The metals rails Bogie sawed off make up the rest of their armoury.

Jimmy organises this second ring of defence, yelling with something approaching Brian's intensity. It's this change in Jimmy that makes Marty suspect the situation is bad. 'Where the fuck is Brian?' Jimmy says. No one knows.

The two dead Typhoons were backs: Flash, the Second Five-Eighth; and Ginger, the Centre. It's a big loss to the team. They had been an awesome midfield combination. Marty loved the lines they ran. Sometimes he received the ball in their scything set movements. Flash would often bust the first tackle and Marty would be on his shoulder. Ginger was a particularly nice guy, and deceptively fast; he had a knack for taking players on the outside. Ginger, Marty's brother-in-arms in the team's hair-based piss-takes, was a reliably happy and affectionate drunk. Someone happy right through. It's a real loss, and one that threatens Marty's hope that the Typhoons will keep playing in Australia, keep winning, keep growing. He has dreamed of them all getting heavy machinery licences and working the mines in summer, then returning to Sydney or Melbourne to play winters. Eventually going to one another's weddings, hanging out with their kids and wives in sunny free prosperity.

Stew puts down his iron rail and vomits into a bag. Marty feels queasy himself; it's only a matter of time before he does the same. We're a pretty feeble safety net, he thinks, looking down the line of players, pale-faced in the night light of the tourist lounge, with their motley collection of iron bars and blades. But we won't be a pushover, he tells himself. Every few minutes now someone pukes. A line has been crossed. He remembers finding himself face down on the lino while the Russians were slaughtered where they sat; how he'd suspected that the blunt force that had floored him was a shot in the back, like the shove a diver once described upon losing a leg to a Great White. Death is close.

He pictures Brian bent over a fresh corpse, looking hard at the face, savouring something inexplicable, shouting in his high-pitched voice.

As well as feeling sick and rotten, Marty is suddenly tired as well. Brian's decisiveness seems superhuman to him. Maybe the price of freedom he's prepared to pay is to let Brian have his way with the tourists with his knife, sniff the life rising out of them, although he suspects that Brian will be worse with women for some reason. He pukes and feels better—but still tired. Very tired. He rests his head on the sofa in front of him.

'Better not sleep, Marty,' Plate tells him.

'True.'

'Be nice though.'

Tunny vomits then lights a cigarette. They watch him turn green and valiantly puff on, slouched against the wall beneath the window.

'Where'd Brian get to?'

'Probably looking for a can opener to attack the Security Centre with.'

'There's a dozen tourists,' says Marty. 'A few chicks too apparently.'

'Love to fuck a Jap,' offers Tunny, who looks on the verge of vomiting again. He groans. 'Oh, that cig was a mistake.' He drops it into the heavy bag.

'I have to say, Brian's "mercy killings" got to me,' says Marty.

Plate grins. 'You yelled at him on the bridge, bro.'

'He practically sawed that dead captain's head off, man. The guy was stone cold dead.'

'Fifteen years in a death camp will do that to you. A lot of his mates were beheaded, eh.'

'Rough justice.' Tunny spits into his bag.

'It'd take me a while to forgive them if you guys were

beheaded,' says Plate.

It's a very real possibility if they're captured at sea, Marty thinks.

Plate is grinning now. 'Australia's going to be sooooo nice, man.'

For the first time Marty suspects they might not make it.

Brian, cat-like, the machine gun he cleared the bridge with slung over his shoulder, makes his way along the back of the barricade, stepping lightly over sleeping and stupefied bodies. The sight of his self-contained lethality immediately restores Marty's faith. The rush of gratitude and wellbeing he feels surprises him. Even his stomach settles.

Brian crouches with them in the dim light. 'I knew you fellas would be awake. The rest of this lot aren't much use.'

They accept the compliment. He's steady, himself again. Marty realises he is vital to them making it, and that the other, bloodthirsty side of him is vital too. His presence is necessary, even if he's just come from torturing women and children.

'Where've you been, Brian?'

'Supervising the diesel transfer.'

'From the trucks?'

'Yes. We siphoned the diesel into barrels and again into jerry cans. A three-hundred-strong chain of men shifted the cans up to the engine room where there's access to the ship's tanks. We've got enough fuel to make it now. As long as those jokers in the Security Centre don't have a say in the matter.'

'Should we attack them?'

'I say yes. The others say no. While we're discussing it, I think they'll have a go—around three or four this morning. In any case, here's some more ammunition.' He demonstrates once again how to load a new magazine. 'Easy. Keep to single shots. A bullet per man is enough.'

It's 2:30. Marty hopes that Brian stays with them, with his sub-machine gun.

'Are you seasick?' Tunny asks him.

'Hard to say,' Brian replies.

Tunny groans and spits into his bag.

'Are there any tourists on board?' Marty asks.

Brian nods wordlessly.

'They could be useful later, as hostages,' Marty suggests.

'They could be useful now,' Brian replies quickly.

'How do you mean?'

Brian takes a metal comb from his back pocket and tugs it through his thick hair until the side parting is cleanly delineated. Normally he would stop combing at this point but he keeps combing.

'Um, the tourists are useful now, Brian?'

Combing, he's miles away. His hand looks old and knotted on the comb. Despite being twenty-odd years older than Marty's father, Eric, Brian is more vital than he and many of the so-called Lost Generation who were born into the most brutal phase of the occupation. Eric has all the appearances of a broken man. He limps, has a bad heart and drinks too much. But he's not broken like some of the vets who made it through the POW camps; it's as if he never formed properly to begin with. Like his growing legs, which were broken in a beating at primary school, he didn't knit together properly. The defects grew larger and made him weak. He learned to be a shadow to escape things, a sweet kind of shadow in his best moments, a grateful shadow.

Tunny vomits.

Brian is animated by hatred, whereas Eric has been worn out and exhausted.

'Wonder if the folks know yet?' Tunny asks.

It's a silly question. The ferry isn't due at Lyttelton until late morning and it's not even 3 am.

'How do you think they'll take the news?' Marty asks him.

'Mum'll cry. Dad'll have a drink.'

'Your dad's home now, eh?'

'Yeah, fucked his elbow. I'm the money-earner now. Gonna send heaps over from Australia.'

'Same, bro,' says Plate.

'Yeah,' Marty says. 'My dad had his legs broken at primary school for speaking English. They've never been right. Even driving's hard for him, eh.'

'He's all right though, your old man.'

'Pretty mellow,' says Marty. 'Never used to hit us or anything. Takes a lot of painkillers.'

'Jesus, that's what my old man needs, morphine for breakfast.'

'Mum basically raised us,' says Tunny. 'She says the old man's a gorilla with a bad heart.'

Their laughter seems to snap Brian into the present.

'I'm going to send the money to me mum,' say Tunny. 'It'll go on piss and gambling otherwise.'

Brian nods.

'You don't drink, do you, Brian?'

'No.'

They wait for him to expand on this exceedingly rare life choice. He doesn't.

'Did you used to?'

'Didn't agree with me.'

Marty sees Brian in a pub toilet, cutting the throat of a man taking a piss at the trough because he said the wrong thing at the bar. 'Good on you,' he says. 'It doesn't agree with a lot of blokes but they keep on drinking.'

'I might have one when all this is over,' Brian says.

'On ya.'

'All right, boys. Wake this lot up. I'll go and check on the front line.'

He's gone, leaving them with their unfired pistols, upturned couches and metal bars.

# Chapter 16:

# The Lord's Angels

Mist turns to drizzle and back to mist. Karori feels like a place of defeat to Chris. Clad in permanent cloud, yet for all its height viewless, it's a basin that looks in on itself, at the road climbing out to a better place. The headquarters of the Lord's Angels is at the far end of the suburb, near the turn-off to Ohariu Valley and the feral fishing community at Makara. The Lord's Angels always set up in places where anti-Japanese sentiment runs highest. In Karori the rentals are very low and few people work. The farmland that once bordered the outermost old and draughty bungalows has been given over to communal vegetable gardens that produce a staple crop of potatoes and onions, vital for trade and survival. Winter is tough. Cases of rheumatic fever, skin infections and respiratory illnesses spike, and there are annual outbreaks of whooping cough. Free New Zealand published the figures for such diseases in Australia: zero; they don't exist. His discomfort grows as he drives further and the houses become shabbier. They're not insulated; paint-peeling, sun-warped, rotten old weatherboards are all that keep out the cold and damp. The Lord's Angels are violent and angry men. He feels he's about to step into a den of lions.

Their headquarters is down a long driveway, hidden from view. He parks on the road, leaving space in front of the car for a quick getaway if necessary. He has brought beer and dressed in black: black jeans, boots and jersey. It's 1 pm and the smell of fishbone stew issues from one of the houses bordering the driveway. He wonders if he looks the part to the curtain-twitchers. Short hair and black clothes: yes. Religious tattoos: no. The look of a life dedicated to racial hatred: maybe. The Lord's Angels will soon see him for what he is. But he has height and beer. The headquarters come into view: it's only a three-bedroom bungalow, four at the most, and he's relieved.

The curtains are drawn and no one answers the door. It's quite possible they aren't up yet. Or only reply to a secret knock. The porch is tidy and he wonders if the headquarters have in fact moved. The house looks normal. He knocks again, and this time a man his age wrenches the door open. Not tall, but broad and strong in his white T-shirt, and covered with religious tattoos. He has a shaven head and a long, beaky nose, which his eyes peer down in puzzlement. Chris notes his woollen socks, which mean he hasn't been out yet. The man looks at him and his beer for a moment. There's something of the vulture about him as he straightens up. With strange precision he places a socked foot on the porch. Standing two steps down, Chris is as tall.

'Gidday,' Chris says.

No reply. The man, quite close, looks over Chris's shoulder. Chris steps back, expecting to see someone. There's no one, and he realises he's being shooed away from the door. The man is definitely not a rugby player, but a boxer. Chris hands him the crate of beer.

'Praise be,' says the man.

134

'I've come for some advice.'

The man turns to go inside and Chris follows. The man stops and Chris stops. He turns his head sideways, showing the long beak of his nose, the broadness of his shoulders and the thickness of his neck, tipped by tattooed wings that Chris guesses belong to the Beast of Revelations. All the while, the same bemused expression in his eyes. He continues into the house and turns into the lounge, Chris a few steps behind in case he stops suddenly again. Another skinhead sits at the end of a brown vinyl couch with a cup of tea and a cigarette. Under his hard face and weight-sculpted frame Chris senses an angry and confused child. There is a large hole in his sock through which Chris glimpses black painted toenails, before the man moves his foot. Or are the nails bruised? The smell of fishbone stew, cigarette smoke and onions permeates the house. The man on the couch glares at Chris as he draws on his cigarette. Probably has me pegged as a prospect, he thinks, the next in line for ritual and improvised humiliation. Two men are behind him now. The man who opened the door stands in the corner in front of the TV, places the crate of beer between his feet, pops one of the bottles with his lighter and hands it to the man on the couch. 'Praise be,' says the benefactor. The man pops another beer, straightens up from his fighter's crouch, tips his head back and drains half the bottle, revealing his powerful biceps and chest as he does so. He has the room's full attention. Back in his fighter's hunch, he regards with his puzzled eyes the men standing behind Chris.

'Don't be a cunt, Narby.' The speaker has an upside-down cross tattooed on his forehead. 'Give us one.'

'You bring those, mate?' says the other to Chris in a hoarse voice.

'Yeah, I want to ask you guys about something.'

Narby stands over the crate, squinting as if dazzled by

the sun.

'Why'd you give Watto one?' says the man with the cross on his forehead.

'Punishment,' declares the man with the hoarse voice.

'Punish him, Narby,' says Watto from the couch with his beer, his hard face cracking gleefully.

Another skinhead comes from the kitchen.

'Who the fuck?' he says to Chris, then sees the beer in the crate at Narby's feet. 'Praise be.'

Narby nods slowly and the newcomer picks up a beer and pops it with his lighter.

'Who the fuck are you?' he repeats, with more feeling, and takes a swig.

At last, Chris thinks, a straight question. 'My name's Chris Ipswitch. My brother is Patrick Ipswitch, the sumo wrestler. He had a kid with a Japanese woman. She was murdered. A three-year-old girl. No one knows who did it. Do you?'

There is a general expulsion of air.

'Fuck me.'

'Who's this wanker?'

'What the fuck?'

All eyes fall on Narby. He walks over to Chris with eyes no longer puzzled but dark and cold. Chris stands his ground, doesn't flinch as Narby stops and straightens in front of him, grabs Chris's balls, and weighs them. Braced for a head butt, every nerve ready to fire, Chris doesn't move.

Narby releases his nuts and turns away.

It's coming, he thinks, and scratches his nose to get his hand up in preparation to block the blow. It doesn't come.

Narby takes a bottle from the crate. 'You've got balls, mate, I'll give you that.' The bottle is the centre of the room's attention. He holds it out. 'Thomson.'

The man with the cross tattooed on his forehead takes it.

'Give it to Roach,' says Narby.

Watto laughs.

'Narby, for fuck's sake,' says Thomson.

'Give it to Roach.'

Thomson hands the bottle over, looking a little pleased despite his ostentatious annoyance. Chris notes he has *The Lord's Angles* tattooed on his forearm.

'You want a beer, Ipdick?' says Narby.

'No thanks. I'll have a cup of tea though.'

Incredulous sounds again. Narby points dramatically to the kitchen.

As Chris fills the kettle to the minimum he feels how hard his heart is thumping in his chest. It's silent in the lounge. A beating is brewing. Or an attempted beating. The jug boils quickly and doesn't switch itself off.

Back in the lounge a circle has formed and each skinhead holds a beer bottle. The most pressing issue, Chris senses, is who will get the last bottle in the crate between Narby's feet, not whether he will be beaten up.

'Cheers,' Chris says from outside the circle. He sips his hot tea.

Another expulsion of air and muttered curses.

Narby grabs his own nuts and turns to focus on Chris. This brings guffaws.

These guys are idiots, Chris thinks, reading Thomson's misspelt tattoo again. They can't tell me anything.

'How'd you get this address?' demands the man who took the beer from the crate himself, whom Chris takes to be Narby's lieutenant.

'A tow-truck driver in Christchurch,' he replies.

'Doober?'

'Yeah.'

'That cunt?'

'My brother put him in hospital a couple of days ago.'

'Hospital,' says Narby.

'Hospital,' repeats Watto.

'Hospital,' echoes Thomson.

Chris knows this is meant to intimidate him, but he doesn't feel weak, he feels strong, like on the rugby field where he never backs down to anyone.

'I hoped you'd know something,' he tells them.

'If we did,' says the lieutenant, 'we wouldn't fucking tell you, would we?'

'Why not?'

Silence.

'I wouldn't go to the police about Christchurch skinheads. I'd take care of it myself.'

They believe him. In actual fact, it's true. He has spoken the truth. He's the tallest in the room and feels his height to be a mighty thing. And he won't fight them and doesn't need to, which is the mightiest thing of all.

'Nothing?' He puts down his empty cup. 'Thanks for the tea. I'll let myself out. Enjoy the brew.' Walking up the driveway he hears Thomson's faint wheedling voice through the window. 'Narby, don't be a cunt.' Gleeful voices rise in unison: 'Punishment!'

# Chapter 17: Mutiny:

# Buried at sea

Some of the mortally wounded ask to be carried up on deck to taste the fresh air. Plate is one of them. At dawn the New Zealand flag can be seen flying on the main mast, and the ship's bow chops like a slow axe towards freedom. When Plate dies after sunrise there are no sheets left for burial shrouds. The best they can manage is three white towels. Five Typhoons have already been shrouded and cast overboard, among a total of 160 dead rugby players. The body count would have been much higher but the Japanese ran out of ammunition. Everyone ran out of ammunition. It came down to knives, bayonets and metal bars, and the losers went overboard, either thrown or jumped. It's the first daylight burial at sea, a dull cloudy morning. Plate's teammates are close to his body; hundreds crowd the surrounding decks. It falls to Brian, who is grey with fatigue, to say a few words.

'It brings us great sadness to lose another good man,' he shouts into the wind, the tissue on his left ear red where the lobe was shot off. 'Plate played a big hand when it looked like we might lose the ship. I'm sorry he didn't get to experience the freedom that was his birthright.' Brian looks up at the New Zealand flag and can manage no more. Marty feels Plate has been let down, that it would have been better that he go in the mass burial performed in pitch darkness a couple of hours after the ship was taken, when every able-bodied man on board performed a mighty haka and they stamped so hard that the ship shook with it.

The Hooker steps forward and lays his arm across Brian's shoulders. Pale, still struggling with seasickness on top of everything else, Bogie begins the Lord's Prayer. 'Although I walk through the valley of death, I fear no evil . . .' Marty remembers the pathetic white packages sliding over the side, one after the other in the dark, so many of them, like grains of rice, all the same in death.

'. . . and forgive us our trespasses,' continues Bogie.

There's a faraway tearing sound. Heads turn to the sky. A jet. Bogie finally ends the prayer, having heard it last of all. 'But deliver us from evil,' he says quietly.

All eyes are skyward as Plate slides overboard. Marty promises himself that he will remember him properly with his surviving friends when they get to Australia, then he scans the sky like everyone else. The thick cumulus is beginning to separate. Deep wells are topped with blue sky. They look to the south, where the jet is coming from. The south. It means only one thing; it starts a stampede. But the crowd is big and the doors small. Marty sees the fighter glint in the sun and change course, bear straight towards them. Curses become cries of terror. Many can only crouch where they are as the jet tears down on them, and over them. By the time the plane turns around, Marty has got to the bow deck where twenty or so wounded lie. Stew is with him. They cannot move their teammates with care because the jet has begun its approach, head-on towards the bow. He counts four rockets slung under the wings as he and Stew carry Kev away from the open space. All of a sudden it comes very fast. He makes himself as small as possible as it screams over the bow. A crackle of small-arms fire becomes apparent as it recedes into the distance. Some of the wounded have been dragged back to consciousness.

'What the fuck was that?' Kev asks.

'A Jap fighter.'

'Oh shit.'

'If the fucker's off a carrier we're fuckin' fucked.'

'Might be alone, Stew. Long-range from Auckland. We aren't sunk yet.' Quietly, so Kev can't hear, he adds, 'We've got the lifeboats, too.'

The fighter has turned and approaches from the port side, low and slow, apparently preparing to fire its rockets at the broadside target, when another jet engine announces itself. A second fighter is coming very fast from the north. Before he can make out any detail, the Mitsubishi fighter abandons its run and activates the afterburner. There's an ear-splitting roar and the sea flattens beneath the fighter as it accelerates into a vertical climb. The newcomer is a Hornet, emblazoned with a red kangaroo in a white-and-blue circle. Marty and Stew punch the air, their cries of joy lost in the roar of the engine as the jet disappears into the cloud in pursuit. As everyone watches and listens, the engines combine and diverge. The Aussie jet appears again in a gap in cloud beyond the stern. It tips its wings in salute, again and again, as it cruises slowly overhead. Marty yells himself hoarse and throws Stew's beanie into the air.

# Chapter 18:

## Cherry Orchard

Monday is usually Chris's big training day. He runs, goes to the gym, swims, and runs again. But now that his team has gone and he won't be playing with them next season, there's no pressing reason to get up and get fit. He's still on the futon at 11 o'clock when the phone rings.

'Hey, Chris . . .'

'What's wrong?'

'Where do I start?'

Chris knows the news must be very bad. He braces himself. 'The worst of it.'

'I'm in prison. Chiyo's missing . . . and . . .'

'What? Patrick? Are you there?'

'It's bad, bro. Her family think I killed her. That I would kill my—' He sobs.

'Pat? Are you there?'

'Can you give me a minute?'

'Sure, sure. Take as long as you need.'

The phone bangs. There's a terrible moan. A scraping sound. 'Ah, she's disappeared, Chris. I don't know where or why. They say I killed her.'

'But . . .?'

'What's happening? I love my wife and child and they blame me. Why the fuck is this happening?'

Chris feels panicky. He can't handle his brother's loss and confusion. It's too big. 'What can I do?'

Patrick has put the phone down again. A roar from a distant room brings hot tears to Chris's eyes. The receiver clunks. 'Chris. I'm losing my mind. Go and see my old master, Mr Ichiro. He might be able to help. If not . . .'

Ninety-eight percent of prosecutions stick, and this means the death penalty. Chris fears suicide as well; his brother has never been so wounded and wild.

'Master Ichiro,' Patrick says. 'You must remember.'

He's a grandfatherly figure in Chris's memory; another Japanese made human long ago by his brother's power. 'Yes, I remember him.'

'Good. See him.'

'Where?'

Patrick takes a deep breath. 'He's over from Japan visiting Cherry Orchard. It's in the paper, that's how I know. We fell out several years ago, but not over race or any of that bullshit.' A ragged breath. Chris fears his brother will break. 'Ask him to come and visit me.' Patrick gathers himself and says clearly and emphatically: 'Or at least call me. He knows everything. He'll be able to tell me what the fuck is going on.'

'I'll go today.'

'Thanks, brother. Tell him I only ever—' His voice trembles. 'I only ever punched with an open hand.'

The line is dead. Chris has never felt so powerless.

The phone rings.

'Pat, listen—'

'Pardon. It's Masuda.'

'Sorry, sir.'

'You are needed here now.'

'Yes.'

The trip to Cherry Orchard will have to wait until tomorrow. His duty is inescapable. It is unthinkable, impossible, to simply not turn up to work after Masuda's call. In order to resign, a month's respectful notice must be given. As he pulls on his suit he reminds himself about the overtime he'll be paid, a strategy he's used in the past when asked to work at inconvenient times, and pictures the silver Akai CS-F11 cassette player with Dolby-B Noise Reduction and digital peak reading display, nearly within his grasp, only two pays away. However, the usual pang of desire fails to materialise. He pictures the sleek slab of silver again, in his apartment this time, on the tatami by his futon. It doesn't work.

As soon as Chris enters the staffroom Masuda stands and his spectacles flash.

'This way,' he grunts.

Chris follows him into one of the small interview rooms. Masuda wheels and shuts the door.

'You are a competent teacher of English. However, we cannot have your family shame reflected on this institution. You will leave immediately. Do your best.'

'Yes.' Chris keeps his eyes down, partly because he doesn't want to see triumph on Masuda's face. 'Please think kindly of me.'

Masuda grunts and is gone.

Chris quickly clears his few personal possessions from his desk. The Wellington Typhoons almanac from last season, when they won the national trophy, is the most important of his belongings. At least he can fulfil his brother's wish and see Master Ichiro today after all. He holds on to this thought. It's early and the other English teachers are yet to arrive, which he's grateful for. He silently bows to the near empty staffroom. His exit goes unnoticed and he knows he will shortly be replaced and forgotten. He realises something he couldn't admit to himself properly an hour ago: his brother will soon be executed.

He tries to enjoy his car as the luxury item it is as he sets off for Cherry Orchard. It will have to be sold after this trip, now that he is unemployed and can't afford to run it. As he heads north on the motorway, the harbour is revealed to be almost entirely brown with sewage and drainwater after the storm. The runoff pipes overflow into the sewerage pipes; the Imperial Japanese Army is not prepared to invest the substantial amount of money required to repair and upgrade the system. I should keep going, he thinks; drive to Auckland and start a new life. But his name, he realises, will follow him everywhere. The only real escape possible is the kind of mission his team mates have attempted. Hijacking the ferry seemed suicidal to him before but now it makes perfect sense. The rewards are potentially huge: freedom; life itself. Failure means only more of the same. He wishes them good luck with all his heart.

For himself, the future holds a trip to Christchurch to be with his brother. He must accompany him throughout the public humiliation of his trial. He must walk with him to his death and dishonour. Chris's eyes fill with tears and he has to pull over. In a dead-end street overlooking the Hutt River he cries for his lost brother, his lost niece, his lost friends, his lost job. He cries for Chiyo too, also dead before her time. Great waves of black and choking despair give way to fear. The future terrifies him, all the long and empty days of his life yet to come without any of the people he loves. The best things in his life have been torn from him. The injustice and the horror of it threaten to crush him and he moans and punches the dashboard.

When he starts the car fifteen minutes or so later, he feels his perspective is clearer. There is little point in going to Cherry Orchard. Better to return to Wellington and make a decent effort to find Bill and get blind drunk with him, as he should have when the ferry went missing. He will lock with Bill in a new team after returning from Christchurch, go to after-matches and meet Kiwi women, live by the sweat of his labour on road and construction gangs, and sabotage the IJA whenever possible. He will live like a New Zealander.

An old woman in a pink tracksuit with a permed helmet of white hair leads a toy dog on a long lead across the road in front of his car. Her transit takes long enough for him to change his mind about returning to Wellington. He switches the indicator to the right instead. I promised Patrick, he thinks. It would not be wise to turn up in Christchurch without trying this one last thing.

After yakitori and a pint of Asahi at the top of the Rimutakas, he feels a little better. The road is not familiar to him because he and his mother always took the train to visit Patrick at Cherry Orchard, and he enjoys the sharp bends and vertiginous aspects. At Featherston he's surprised at how unchanged everything is. Cherry Orchard itself—though a big complex, with many rooms and halls for trainees, instructors and bottom division wrestlers—looks basically the same from the road, but for a big tourist bus. The stable became famous after Patrick left. As he drives through the open gate Chris feels positive associations. It was a friendly place when he came here as a child. He and his mother were always warmly received by the master, even when Patrick was being punished.

'Welcome to Cherry Orchard Stable, sir,' says the receptionist. He asks her if it would be possible to see Master

Ichiro, and tells her his name and his relationship to Rising Dragon, the famous wrestler from this very stable. 'Patrick Ipswitch,' he tells her blank face. 'He was popularly known as the Night Train.' The girl becomes very respectful and says she will do everything in her power to contact the master. She suggests he take a tour in the meantime; it began only five minutes ago and he will be able to join it in the wrestlers' dining room. Chris knows where the dining room is. On his way there he hears the distinctive clip clop of wooden sandals worn by junior trainees. Three Maori boys of about fourteen come into view, clad in thin cotton robes, the full extent of their winter wardrobes. They're still slim. Such junior trainees had seemed like men to him when he first visited Cherry Orchard as a child of six. He stops and watches them clip-clop down the path towards the kitchen door, probably on their way to peel potatoes. They will have been up since 5 am. Such a life once appeared glamorous to him. Potential must have been at the heart of it, the possibility of going all the way—to Japan, the top divisions, fame and fortune. He can still feel some of Patrick's old ambition, and remembers sharing his contempt for those who dropped out. The boys disappear into the building and Chris stands for a moment, trying to understand what has happened to his brother, when he feels he is being watched.

A white-haired Japanese man in a black suit stands on the path fifty metres away, staring. It's Master Ichiro. He has aged greatly in the passage of the dozen years since Chris last saw him. Chris waves and smiles and makes his way eagerly towards him. As he draws near he apologises, bows, and introduces himself, and a funny thing happens: age falls away from the master. His colour returns and his back straightens.

'Little Ipswitch. You came too late. I needed you at sixteen. I believe you promised me that.'

147

'Forgive me, Master. I was wiser at eight than I am now.'

'We all unlearn the wisdom of childhood. Some faster than others.'

Chris takes this as a criticism of Patrick and is unsure how to respond other than by agreeing.

'I always thought you'd be a better wrestler than your brother.'

Chris checks for a twinkle in the old master's eye. To his great surprise, there isn't one.

'Your brother sent you.'

'Yes, Master.'

'I thought you were him: sixteen again and starting out. I thought he had come to say goodbye to Cherry Orchard and maybe to me.'

'A ghost? Is . . . has my elder brother . . . died?'

'Apparently not.' The colour has returned to the master's face.

'I spoke to him today, Master, on the phone.'

'Good! We'll drink tea.'

'Thank you. Thank you very much for your time.'

Master Ichiro leads him to the tourist canteen rather than his private rooms, and Chris is disappointed. They take a seat in the corner and a small pot of tea is placed before them. Only enough for one cup each. He fills the cups and waits for the master to speak.

'Your brother made Grand Champion at the youngest age ever. Now he finds himself alone.'

'Yes, Master, and unsure of his crime.'

'Well . . .'

'My brother lost many friends in this country when he had a child. Many in Japan resented him for becoming Grand Champion. Of all the friendships he lost, it is yours he regrets most, Master.'

The master sips his tea. 'What is his message?'

148

'I don't understand it, Master. He said to tell you that he only ever hit with an open hand.'

'I wanted you, younger Ipswitch, but your mother wouldn't give both her sons to me to fatten up. I hoped for a third brother, to free you for sumo, but he never came.'

'I . . . uh . . . me?'

'Your brother is innocent?'

'Foolishly,' Chris says, 'he married for love. He didn't think his child with Chiyo was a crime. Just unusual.'

'Just unusual. Well.'

'My niece was a lovely little girl, Master. Yet I've heard even the Emperor disapproved of her. And the New Zealand public disapproved of her. I think they never saw her smile. And Chiyo as well.'

'Your older brother thinks it's political?'

'Yes.'

'No, it's personal.'

A chill runs down Chris's spine.

'Who of the top tier have come to his aid?'

'I don't know, Master. I only met Noble Dawn. He mentioned—'

'Yes, Noble Dawn. You need look no further. Your brother made him very . . . angry.'

Chris pictures the gentle giant sipping tea with Chiyo at his brother's house. He had her killed as well? Or did it himself? It doesn't make sense. 'Noble Dawn is behind this?'

'Believe me. Now, his mana and power are great in Japan, but somewhat less here, somewhat less. I suggest you talk to him in a public place before going to the police, or at least threatening him with the police.'

'The police?'

'Yes, the police here will not be quite so easy to buy out and are probably completely unaware of his role in these murders. This threat of yours may well be enough. The processes in motion against your older brother can be halted by Noble Dawn, I believe, without him having to confess.'

'Thank you, Master. I will talk to him. But why has he done this?'

The Master nods and stands. 'Noble Dawn will be judging at the sumo tournament in Auckland beginning on Monday. Approach him there and suggest he's had revenge enough. And of course you haven't spoken to me. This last point is important.'

'Of course I will not mention you, Master. You have my word.'

'I've said enough. Goodbye, young man, and good luck.'

The conversation is over. Chris stands, bows deeply, thanks the Master and maintains his deep bow until he has left the dining room. His mind whirls. He doesn't see anything as he heads for the exit. The most pressing thing, he decides, is whether to continue on to Auckland immediately or return home first. Lost in agitated thought he takes three wrong turns while returning to his car.

# Chapter 19: Mutiny:
# Brian has a celebratory

The Typhoons meet in the lounge they successfully defended against two attacks, the second being a samurai sword charge. They don't notice the blood-soaked carpet and walls as they relive the defence: the doorway piling with bodies from the loosies' crossfire, the grenades, thrown by the enemy, that very fortunately exploded in front of the barricade of tables, and then the hand-to-hand combat on the decks after the ammunition ran out and the hunt for the last terrified soldiers in the bowels of the ship. The arrival of the jets is celebrated again and the New Zealand flag rising skyward, step by step, to the top of the highest mast; and then the mighty haka during the burial ceremony is remembered.

Brian's arrival breaks a prolonged silence. Everyone remembers they've made it. Their enthusiastic greeting dislodges a rare smile from the man. Before long, though, he's nodding distractedly in reply to questions. He seems smaller and older to Marty, and less present, as if the other dimension he sees has grown more engaging. Marty guesses that the gun slung over his shoulder is empty. Unconsciously, still absent, he begins working his comb through his hair, and like a spell, it brings him back into focus. 'Is your hand okay, son?' he asks Tunny.

'Shithouse,' Tunny replies cheerfully, 'but I'm not complaining. I've stopped puking.'

'Show me. Look, come with me, I might have something for that. Marty, you too.'

Brian leads them away from the team. They are chosen ones. For a moment Marty allows himself to feel proud.

'Have you got some anaesthetic for it, Brian?' Tunny's voice is hopeful as they descend into the ship and make their way to the tourist cabin area.

'Something like that,' Brian replies, without looking around.

As they pad down the carpeted corridor, Marty worries that Brian is taking them to the captive female tourists for a 'treat', a reward for being the gunmen. When Brian stops at a cupboard, unlocks it and pulls out a bottle of Johnny Walker Red, a strong sense of relief mixes with gratitude.

'You legend,' whispers Tunny, awestruck.

It's a top-shelf whisky, one which Marty's never tried.

'I felt like a quiet drink now it looks like we'll make it, but didn't want to drink alone,' Brian says. 'It's been many years,' he adds.

'Too many, Brian. Thanks for thinking of us.'

'Well, you boys deserve it. You did a wonderful job.'

'You've even got glasses,' Tunny says.

'Three will have to do. I would have preferred five. It's a damn shame Jimmy and Plate can't be with us.'

'Our first toast should be to them,' Marty says. He wants Jimmy and Plate and the other lost Typhoons to be remembered properly. That's what he wants from the bottle. Not sentimentality but focus.

Brian unlocks a tourist cabin. It's small but sleek and plush, and hints at the larger luxuries enjoyed by the Japanese in

New Zealand. 'All right for some,' Brian says as he places the bottle and glasses on the little table between the two single beds. The sheets have not been stripped for shrouds. Marty and Tunny sit on the bed opposite him.

'A standard cabin,' Brian says bitterly.

Tunny has eyes only for the whisky. 'Great timing, Brian. I just stopped puking this morning.'

'So you said,' Brian replies. He fills the tall glasses to the brim, as if the whisky were beer.

'No mercy,' Marty says.

'It's been a while since you've had a drink?' Tunny asks.

'It has.'

Tunny discreetly elbows Marty in the ribs. The nudge is not nearly discreet enough, in Marty's opinion. Brian is in a strange, deliberate mood.

'To freedom?' With a flourish, Brian attempts to down the entire glass, but almost immediately he splutters and coughs.

To save Brian's honour, Marty and Tunny drink until they gag. Seeing Brian's weepy eyes and red face they exaggerate their coughing and suffering. Embarrassingly, Brian's eyes may not be watering, but weeping. It's not yet the time to cry; they're not drunk.

'Here's to Jimmy,' Brian says, with unambiguous feeling. This time, astonishingly, he finishes the tall glass. Tears are rolling down his cheeks as Marty and Tunny slam theirs down. He immediately pours another round.

'Hang on,' Marty says. 'I need a minute.'

'To the dead,' Tunny says, despite his very empty stomach.

Marty drinks even though he knows it will not stay down. Brian stops mid-glass and chucks on the bunk right next to where he sits. Once, twice, three times. It's brown liquid. The whisky's come straight back up.

'Another,' he says, 'to rinse my mouth out.'

'Hard-fucking-core, mate,' Tunny says. He finishes his second glass and abruptly stands. Thankfully, he makes it to the en suite.

This is ludicrous, Marty thinks. 'Look, we should slow down a bit.'

'To the dead!' Tunny cries into the toilet bowl.

Marty stands and drinks and swings into the en suite, where he is obliged to vomit into the basin because Tunny's still retching over the toilet. When they return to the table Brian is sitting solemnly by his puddle of vomit. He pours another round.

'Mayhem,' Marty says.

Brian begins silently and stoically weeping. Tunny places a hand on the older man's shoulder as Brian drinks again, only a sip this time. They gratefully follow his lead. Lacing his fingers on the table, Brian takes a deep breath. Having had a drink, he is ready to speak. 'There's nothing for me in Australia.'

'No way!'

'Don't say that, Brian,' Marty cries. 'Jesus, you'll finally be free!'

'You young fellows are starting out. You'll quickly put down roots, start families of your own. I can't do that anymore.'

'You're still young, Brian. Everyone thinks that.' In fact Brian looks much older than he ever has and has the pallor of someone badly wounded.

'My roots are in New Zealand.'

'There are other old fellas on board,' Tunny says. He's slurring now, the drunkest of the three.

'What will we do?'

'Fuck, I dunno. What do old fellas do? Gardening and tinkering. Home brew. Excuse me.'

The cabin reeks of vomit. Tunny's new bout of noisy

154

retching makes Marty want to laugh but he can't offend Brian. He must not laugh while this warrior opens his heart to them. Not only is it disrespectful, but it may be fatal. He suspects Brian may lash out uncontrollably if offended. But the vomit, Tunny's comical high-pitched retching, the abruptly three-quarters-empty bottle . . . he coughs to disguise a giggle.

'You're laughing at me,' Brian says. His expression is chilling.

'No,' Marty says emphatically. 'I'm laughing at the mayhem.' And he's aware of the space between him and Brian, and that he's within knife range.

'Mayhem,' Brian repeats with the trace of a sneer.

The brown puddle of vomit next to Brian is now very unfunny. It is the man's pain. It is their pain.

'I'm what they use to call "a mean drunk" in the old days, Marty. I came here with you two because I respect you and felt I could trust myself. But now I find you don't respect me.'

'Hang on. That's not true Brian. We do—'

'Flash Harrys,' Brian says, clenching his jaw. Marty feels a terrible judgement has been passed, one which will cost him and Tunny dearly. He feels weak.

'You're a fuckin' legend, Brian,' Tunny announces from the bathroom door, 'but this is a pretty unusual way of tackling a bottle of whisky, I have to fuckin' say. Don't you think?'

Brian's red eyes close. He appears to be counting to himself, and Marty finds the strength to stand and take a step towards the toilet. 'Well, yes,' Brian finally replies, looking up to where he and Tunny stand in the doorway, ready to shut the door on him if necessary. He seems unsurprised, as if they've taken a perfectly sensible precaution. 'It's been thirty years, lads. I don't go to bars for a reason. That whisky

. . . surprised me.'

'Thirty years since you've had a drink?'

'You have to understand . . . I've killed a lot of men. I don't remember how many. I need to pay attention.'

'We've killed men too, Brian.'

He nods. His thick hair is still neatly styled but his colour is very bad. The shot-off earlobe has been replaced by a clotted red clump of toilet paper. To Marty he looks both noble and evil, a transitional being who could emerge black or white. He narrows his eyes and says thickly, 'I'm going to miss being at war.'

A gallant admission, Marty thinks; a good sign. 'You can fight for New Zealand in Australia, Brian.'

'Diplomacy.' The word clearly disgusts him. Marty sees the man that licks the blood of corpses. He knows he must avoid platitudes because Brian is like a mad snake ready to strike at anything, no matter how innocuous. There is the ridiculous possibility that he might die in this vomit-filled cabin, when so close to freedom. He shuts his mouth and stares at the table top. The sound of a jet engine filters into the cabin, approaching from the direction of the bow, from the north. It gives Marty an excuse to put some distance between himself and Brian. He shuffles along the bed to the cabin window and tries to catch a glimpse of a red kangaroo insignia, but the jet passes out of sight. Unwilling to face Brian, he keeps looking out the window at the breaking clouds.

'The weather's definitely clearing,' he says.

'The weather. Hot weather. Dry weather. Fucking Australia.'

Brian never swears. Ever. Marty is now certain that things will end badly. He wants Tunny back, who is trying the bathroom tap for at least the third time. The ship's been dry for hours yet each time a tap doesn't work he is freshly annoyed, as if the lack of water is a considered denial, a personal insult. The top of the cistern comes off with a clatter, and Marty quells an urge to laugh at the sounds of the big drunk man in a small bathroom. Tunny cheers for the jet as he yanks on a roll of toilet paper.

'Woohoo,' Brian echoes sourly, as if Tunny's expression of joy was not manly. He blinks slowly and grits his teeth.

Feeling that Brian is about to move, Marty takes the bottle as if to top up the glasses. Brian is up and out. His sudden exit is a great relief, like a gust of fresh air.

'Phew . . .'

'Jesus, where'd he go?' Tunny asks, head around the bathroom door, more alert than Marty would have thought possible.

'Gone to cause trouble.'

'Mate, I thought he was going to have a go. I was ready for it. Was gonna use the top of the dunny as a shield.'

'I think he's going for the tourists.'

'Mate . . .'

They stumble out of the vomit-smelling cabin. The corridors are empty. Everyone is on deck in the brightening weather watching the Aussie jets. They don't know where to look, and even if they should find Brian, Marty knows it could cost them their lives to try stopping him now. He's just about convinced himself to go up on the top deck when a woman's muffled scream comes from nearby. Only one locked and windowless cabin is the possible source. They wait, frozen. They hear a whimper, and a woman say, 'No.'

Tunny pulls ineffectually at Marty's arm. 'I'm wasted,' he says. 'I can't take Brian on. He's a fuckin' killer. We get help or leave him to it.'

'No,' says Marty, standing solid despite the sensation of his strength leaving him. 'We can appeal to him, through the door.'

'Appeal? It's not cricket. And I don't know if I care,' says Tunny. 'No Japanese chick ever stuck up for me when I was being beaten up.' He attempts to shepherd Marty away.

Marty shakes him off and knocks loudly on the door. 'Brian. It's Marty.'

A Japanese woman's accented English: 'Help us!'

Another: 'Help!'

'Oh!'

With a sinking, hopeless feeling, Marty knocks louder. 'Brian? Let us in. Me and Tunny want a go!'

Tunny shakes his head and joins Marty at the door. 'Are you fucking crazy?' he hisses. Marty sees his own fear reflected in his friend's eyes. Yet something makes him knock again.

Through the door comes Brian's voice; it sounds as if he has something in his mouth. 'You young buggers stay away.'

The women's voices rise in terror. Children begin wailing. Marty can't make out what they're saying in the sudden clamour. Panicked, he changes tack. 'We all have a future, Brian. You and those mothers and children too.' His words sound hollow, useless. A full-blooded scream turns him away. He can't listen. He walks away, leaving Tunny at the door, and climbs out of the carpeted tourist area, up to the top deck and the sun. He leans on a rail, squinting, and feels drunk and heavy. The engine roars through a nearby vent. The ship seems to slide over the waves. The air's different; it's warmer. Australia will be sunny. Tunny's absence is awful. *No, I can't do it. I can't leave him, can't leave defenceless people to be knifed and slaughtered.* He returns below deck on rubbery legs, into the dim, carpet-muffled, blood-stained corridors. Tunny's on his knees on the floor; his broad back bent over Brian's bloody corpse. The dead man's tear-filled eyes stare at nothing, truly nothing this time. There will be no coming back. His knotty hands grip Tunny's hands.

Tunny turns and looks up. His eyes are full of tears too. 'He cut his own throat, Marty. He stopped himself, bro.'

Muffled sobbing comes from the cabin. He opens the door on a TV room; its plush leather couches are crowded with terrified women and children. It's hot and stinks of sweat, urine, excrement and some other powerful odour. The women, a dozen of various ages, shrink back. Those with children draw them closer. Pale, their hair plastered to their skulls, stripped down to T-shirts, barefoot, they won't look at him, but stare at the floor instead.

'Okay?' he asks. A black puddle of blood is smeared under the door. No one is cut; no one is bleeding to death. It must be Brian's blood. 'Okay?' he asks again. The women seem afraid to breathe. Tunny chokes a sob in the corridor. 'Sorry,' Marty hears himself saying. 'He was an old soldier . . . a man who fought for his country for too long . . .' They want him to go. He closes the door. A jet howls low overhead, and from the top deck a ragged cheer goes up. A puff of fresh warm air finds its way to him. They've made it.

# Chapter 20:

# From Featherston to Waiterere

Chris wakes curled up in the back seat of his car with a dry tongue and pulsing head. His neck is sore. It's 2:07 in the morning and pitch black outside. The darkness is partly due, he discovers upon getting out of the car, to the huge old macrocarpa he's parked under: the old king in a line of pines along the gravel road. Water flows on the other side of the trees. The air is mild. And although he feels like shit, he's grateful the spinning has stopped. His eyes adjust and the icy gleam of a wide and fast-flowing creek flashes through the pines. Negotiating his way down the bank, he sits abruptly in a bed of pine needles. Still wasted, he thinks, and steps with exaggerated care on the stones of the creek bed. The swiftly flowing water flares strangely at its edges. Phosphorus, he thinks. No, the word comes to him: fluorescence. A lot of hash was smoked. He takes off his T-shirt and sits on a boulder to remove his jeans. The water he splashes over his head and chest is violently, gaspingly cold. He kneels at the water's edge summoning the courage for another splash. His last act at the Port Ferry Hotel was climbing out of a toilet window to escape . . . what was her name? Turza? He wonders how long she waited outside the door for him. It was bad form to run off like that, but probably didn't cause her lasting pain, given how wasted she was and the interest a couple of other guys had shown in her. There was nothing wrong with her, really, other than she didn't have the poise and grace of Hitomi Kurosawa. He didn't say goodbye to his host either, the barman, a nice guy who played pool with him while the bar was quiet, shouted him a jug and took him out back into the kitchen for a spot of hash on the stove. From that point things are hazy. A couple of the barman's mates showed up, and Turza, and a couple more women, and suddenly it was dark and very sociable. At some point he realised he was no longer a conscious actor. It was a brief moment of lucidity as he took the hot knives from the element and one of his new friends dropped a clump of hash onto the red-hot metal. A burst of smoke which he sucked into the sawn-off milk container someone else held at his lips—and he had gone under again, operating on pure instinct, which was exactly what he wanted.

He strips naked and wades out up to his thighs. It's better, he remembers, to drink the fast-flowing water near the centre. 'Careful, careful,' he tells himself. The sensation of ice around his legs loosens its grip. The creek is merely very cold. He wobbles, takes a step backwards and abruptly sits down. Gasping, he puts his head under. And again. Sitting naked in the freezing creek he drinks his fill and then wonders what to say to Noble Dawn when he finds him. The lights of a car downstream mark a bridge and the main road. 'What has my brother done?' he asks the freezing water rushing away with his body heat to the sea. No answer comes. I will appeal to Noble Dawn's reason, he thinks, to his compassion. He stands and loses his balance. He hits the water and a river stone turns under his hand. His head goes under for a second. The water feels a bit warmer.

Maybe the sea is warm too. He has a feeling people are waiting for him downriver. His niece, his mum, the father he never knew, Johnny Lennon.

'Testicles are not overrated.'

'Huh?'

It's Johnny Lennon's voice, muffled. It's hard to tell if the figure under all the oversized fur-and-leather polar gear is him; his face is hidden in the hood's long dark tunnel and his outfit is so ridiculously bulky he can barely move. The tips of his mittens, of the old-school variety Scott wore, but fifty sizes too big, trail along the stones. 'Eunuchs are said to miss theirs most in the morning,' he says. 'I'm not going downriver to retrieve them for you, I can tell you that now, young man. So out you get. Speedo, speedo.'

'Ah, piss off. You're imaginary.'

'Said Aladdin to the genie.'

'Aladdin is also imaginary.'

'Stop talking to me and listen, you fuckin' idiot. You won't be of any help to your brother if you die in this creek. And listen, I'm not picking my nose down by the sea with your relatives waiting for your corpse to show up. You have a duty to the living, man. Do you want your dad's phantom foot up your phantom arse? That's what's waiting for you if you sit there much longer. Get up and get out of this fucking creek!'

A shiver of embarrassment penetrates Chris's warming body. He lurches to his knees. 'But, I—'

Johnny puts on the voice of an exasperated old woman. 'Shut up and put some clothes on.'

'Okay.' Chris lurches alarmingly; his balance has gone and he hits the water twice on the few steps it takes to return to the bank. His numb feet strike stones as he carries his clothes, jaw chattering. The carpet of pine needles barely registers. He sits in the passenger seat with the engine

162

running and heater blasting.

Lennon knocks soundlessly on the glass with a giant seal-fur mitten. Chris winds the window down.

'You were right about the genie in one sense, Chris. I've seen you twice and will come one more time.'

'Thanks, Johnny.'

'Good, you're bowing again. A sure sign you're feeling better. Get warm, brother. Time to roll.'

Johnny manages a thumbs-up sign with the massive mitten, curls into a ball and rolls and bounces away down the road as if he's inflated with air. Chris can't help but smile at this exuberant exit, even though he's sorry to see Johnny go. The warmth of his presence remains. Once dry he moves out of the wet seat, gets dressed and, still shivering sporadically, sets off for the drive back to Wellington over the Rimutakas.

It's after 3 when he lets himself into his apartment. After turning on the shower he strips and looks in the fridge. Exhausted, seeking to hit his futon as quickly as possible, he is about to take two chicken drumsticks into the shower when there comes a sharp knock on the door. Through the bending, shrinking lens of the peephole he sees a woman's blond hair. He bites the drumstick in his right hand and wonders. She knocks again and he opens the door.

'Oh.' Hitomi's face flashes. 'Breakfast?' she asks, looking at the drumsticks in his hands.

'Dinner. Just got home.'

'May I come in?'

'Please.'

She steps in and, as the heavy door closes behind her, kneels and kisses the end of his dick, then takes the head in her warm mouth. He finishes the drumstick in his right hand and tears into the other. Turza would have done this, he thinks, if I'd opened the toilet door. She just wanted to do this good thing. What an odd misunderstanding. He lobs the drumsticks into the sink. He would touch Hitomi's head but his fingers are greasy and would mark her wig. A strange current of regret and sorrow rushes through him as he comes. She gags, surprised no doubt by how quickly it happened. My dick's still stoned, he thinks.

'Lovely to see you, Hitomi,' he says, pulling her to her feet and hugging her. She nods and blinks, unwilling to speak or open her mouth. 'Here, I put the kettle on for you. I'll just hop in the shower.'

Only in the shower does he wonder how she found him. Why would she come so late on a weeknight? The answer is that she's like Turza and he is paranoid.

She lies on her back under the covers in his single futon. Her bare shoulders indicate she is at least topless. He turns off the light.

'I like the wig, but you can take it off.'

'I'll always wear it when we're together. It must become a habit. Until I dye my hair blond, right?'

'Okay.'

She's so slim they can both fit on the single futon.

'Plenty of room.'

He runs his hand lightly over her, checking she's naked.

'How did you find me?'

'You told me your address. I remembered the building but not the number so clearly. I thought it was 12 or 22. The woman in 12 thought I was a prostitute. She was very rude, yeah? Then I tried 22.'

'Why so late?'

'So no one sees me.'

'Hitomi, I've been fired.'

'Oh?' She raises herself on her elbow. It takes an effort to open his eyes. Concern is etched over her imperious

164

face. The blond hair makes her non-racial, a kind of perfect model human. And she's nude in his lonely bed. He ignores the first twinge of sexual excitement. 'Why?' she asks.

'Family scandal. I'll tell you tomorrow. I'm shattered.'

Her fingers stroke his head. 'Your hair's getting long.'

'I'm going to Auckland tomorrow morning.'

'Why?'

'To see a man about a dog.'

'I see.'

He's grateful that she understands.


She's shaking him. 'Wake up. Wake up.'

The electric clock reads 5:30 am. He feels he's only just dropped off.

'Let's go,' she tells him, throwing back the covers. She stands over him, naked but for the wig, with a commanding hand on her hip. His dick stirs.

'No time for that,' she says, pointing to it. 'I'm coming with you as far as the Kapiti coast. If we leave now in the dark you can drop me off there.'

He wants to fuck her now and leave in a leisurely fashion later, alone.

'Sit on this.'

'I'll sit on it at the bach. Now get up.' She turns away and dresses rapidly.

'You have a bach to stay at?'

'Yes. My friend gave me the key to use any time.'

Half an hour later she is standing in a corner of the underground car park as he throws his pack in the boot of his car and hangs his suit in the back window. It will provide some cover, if nothing else. As soon as she gets in the car she reclines the seat and closes her eyes. He feels jealous.

He knows he shouldn't, but he stops for a coffee at the kiosk outside the railway station, leaving her asleep in the car park. The first trains have arrived in darkness. He returns to the car with the coffee and sees her sleeping face partly illuminated in the harsh street light. An attractive Japanese woman in a wig. At least his lateish-model car is appropriate, a good fit for her. Commuters march past, their hard-soled shoes striking the pavement with military urgency. He knows it was risky to stop, but he's very grateful for the coffee as he pulls away.

He recalls Master Ichiro suggesting that he would have made a great wrestler. Strangely, perhaps, it was never an ambition of his, despite having the kind of height and width that would fill out well. Maybe it was the thought of living in his brother's shadow that stopped him, he thinks; the impossibility of matching his achievements. Still, he's flattered. As the caffeine takes effect, the possibility of going to the national sumo tournament in Auckland, finding Noble Dawn there and reasoning with him, becomes real and easily achievable. He remembers Master Ichiro saying that Noble Dawn had the power to stop the prosecution without having to confess anything himself, that Noble Dawn had the power to singlehandedly release Patrick and restore him to his previous position. The chain of misfortune can be turned off like a tap. Because the murder is a personal vendetta rather than the act of a political institution, Patrick is caught in a single strand rather than a web and can be released much more easily. In the coffee glow, his intention to talk to Noble Dawn man to man seems exactly right; to let him know in a subtle way that his revenge (well-deserved, Chris will admit, even though he has no idea what offence Patrick could possibly have committed to justify the murder of an innocent child and her mother) has gone far enough, and to suggest that the door is now open to him, Noble Dawn, the victor, to end hostilities mercifully before the police are alerted. And if the mention of the police doesn't

166

faze him, maybe Chris's threat of going to Free New Zealand will. The coffee is finished but its encouraging effect lingers. His plan feels inspired, rational, reasonable, and its success inevitable. The key thing, Chris concludes, is to get the man alone. Everything else will follow.

Hitomi wakes at the Paremata roundabout as the eastern sky begins to lighten. It's a dull and cloudy day. The water in the middle of the inlet pales while headlights float around its dark edges.

'You should probably stay down in the built-up areas.' He's speaking English. 'Keep your head down in the towns, I mean.'

'Mmm.'

'Where's the bach?'

'I can't say it very well. Waiterere Beach.'

'Your Maori pronunciation's better than mine.'

'Same vowel sounds, yeah? Vow-els. Vow-els,' she says, as if there's a ball rolling in her mouth. 'Hah.'

'Have you been to the bach before?'

'No. I have the address. My friend gave me a key and said to use it any time.'

'But what about your job?'

'Ha. I told you last night but you fell asleep in one second. Bang.'

'Okay. What did you tell me?'

'I quit.'

'Why?'

'I don't need the money—that much. It's Mazda, but not really Mazda. I think this is a Japanese thing.'

'In Japanese?'

'This lifelong commitment to the company we Japanese enjoy has its advantages if the company is strong. But there's no real market here for Mazda. No opportunity for expansion, right? The company basically supplies maintenance to an ageing fleet. It's a different mindset in New Zealand. A man would be ashamed to drive a car more than five years old in Japan. Here, even company cars are often more than seven years old. Kiwis drive twenty-year-old cars. Mazda here is basically a used-car dealer. I ran around like some kind of weird nurse selling overpriced parts for dying cars. The idiots I had to deal with—'

'You speak a lot faster in Japanese.'

'Of course. It's my mother tongue.'

'Obviously. Not all Japanese speak as quickly as you though.'

'The Japanese here . . . their vocabularies shrink. They speak in a very functional and practical way. It's almost a dialect. A dialect lacking the vocabulary to articulate abstractions, right? I got sick of men talking to me about rust and rugby. A really smart guy would say "corrosion".'

'I fear I may not be smart enough for you, Hitomi.'

'Fear? I don't think you know the meaning of the word.'

As they enter the outskirts of Levin, she turns sideways in her seat, away from the window. At a red light in the centre of town, she shrinks down while farmers and shopkeepers cross the road in front of them intent on their destinations. Random checkpoints for morning commuters are rare, but it occurs to Chris for the first time since leaving his apartment that they could be stopped at any time. He has made the trip in a hungover fog, high on caffeine, with no plan at all on how to deal with a checkpoint. However, if his foolishness has come across as bravery, he'll take the credit.

As they turn off onto the gravel road that leads to the beach, she consults a scrap of paper and gives directions. The sky is light grey. A thick belt of pines lies behind the dunes. The further they drive down the potted road parallel to the sea, further from the main road and little cluster of shops, the better Chris feels. The baches become scattered. They reach the very end of the road and turn into a dead end bordered by pines. There are only three baches and theirs is the most secluded, hard against the pines with private access to the beach.

'Perfect.'

Even the driveway, running down the seaward side of the house, is private; with access to the door it means they can get out of the car and unload entirely out of view of the other baches. Stretching in the pale light, she nods approvingly.

'Very isolated,' she says. 'Like my friend said.'

He likes the fresh scent of the pines too, the sea's dull roar, and the prospect of getting laid in a leisurely fashion. He's wondering if he should stay until dark before continuing on to Auckland, when he spots the squat shape of a sumo figurine in the long grass under a straggly apple tree. In a moment he has the heavy ball-shaped object in his hands. It's his brother, fired to a glossy finish and looking almost Japanese with his black topknot. But the almond eyes and features are unmistakeably Patrick's. Chris laughs as he turns the figure over, delighted by the craftsmanship. It strikes him as being a very good omen. Maybe a sign he should stay a while.

'My brother,' he says proudly, replacing the figure under the tree.

'Great.' She looks as happy as he's ever seen her. She tries the key and the door swings open.

'You didn't bring anything,' he says, stepping inside with his bag.

She stops him in the doorway and kisses him. It's a serious kiss and he's not sure why it should be solemn. He'd prefer to celebrate.

'It's dry,' he says.

'Dry?'

'These places can be damp,' he says cheerfully, looking

over her shoulder into the brown lounge. Hitomi's friend is a Kiwi, he sees. The few books are English language dating from pre-1943 and post-1985. Mainly there are board games and video cassettes. He finds that the fridge and hot water are on. She watches him do his round and drop his bag in the bedroom with the queen-size bed.

'I put something in your bag,' she says.

He finds his hair-clippers. There is an extension cord in the laundry and she cuts his hair outside in a sheltered corner. It's the first time they've been out in the light of day together. She wears her blue sunglasses, gumboots and a plastic cooking apron for the occasion. She laughs often as she dabs very cautiously at his hair with the clippers, and intersperses her laughter with apologies. 'Oh, no . . . sorry . . . I hope you'll be able to forgive me . . . whoops.' He finds her laughter to be very Japanese in this regard.

'We'd better wait until dark for the beach,' he says.

'The haircut's not that bad!'

He laughs.

'Have you had a good day, sir?' she says in English.

He turns around. She's pretending to look at a mirror in front of them.

'Good, thanks. I ran away with my Japanese girlfriend.'

She resumes cutting his hair with microscopic movements. 'Is she really your girlfriend?'

'Yes, she just doesn't know it yet.'

'Oh . . . she must be crazy.'

'That's what I like about her.'

She puts the clippers on the ground and walks quickly away, clomping in the big gumboots. The clippers keep buzzing as he wonders what to do. He runs his hand over his head. It's very uneven.

170

# Chapter 21:

## Someone's crazy

She's standing over the sink watching the tap run. The gumboots, apron and blue sunglasses are gone.

'Hitomi.' He can see she's trembling. 'Look at me.' He means his half-shaved head, a winning card, surely. As she turns he smiles.

'Don't call me crazy.'

'I won't.' Raising his hands he moves toward her.

'You did though, just now.'

'You said it first. I thought we were joking. You know, the invisible hairdressing salon.'

'Uh.' She scoots away from him to the lounge area on the other side of the kitchen bench and fixes him with a blank expression. He sits down on a bench stool. She continues to stand. 'You imagine your life is perfect,' she says, 'that you do everything exactly as you should. You think—'

He cuts her off. 'No. Things are very bad for me now.' He's tempted to suggest she is crazy. His car is right there, through the sliding door.

'That's the reason you want to see me.'

'Of course. Shelter in a storm.'

'Shelter? I don't think you mean that. You're saying that just to make amends.'

'You think my life's some kind of paradise? Don't you listen when I speak to you? My niece has been murdered. My brother is in prison, about to be charged with his wife's murder. I lost my job. My team has drowned at fucking sea. Maybe you are crazy—'

She blinks. 'You're so calm and collected. It's as if all those things were minor inconveniences. You're going to Auckland to buy a dog! As if that will fix everything.'

'What?'

'You told me you're going to buy a dog in Auckland.'

Nuts. Obviously. As he stands to leave, he remembers. 'That's an English idiom!' In English he says: 'I'm going to see a man about a dog means I have some business to attend to.'

'What?'

'I did say that. It's just a weird expression.'

'You don't have to go to Auckland?'

'Yes, for business. I haven't had the chance to tell you.'

'You don't tell me anything because you think I'm crazy!' In a moment she's out the door and running for the pines. In broad daylight.

He takes the clippers to the bathroom and finishes the haircut inside five minutes. It's time to cut down to essentials, he realises, as his hair falls way. He needs to go to Auckland and speak to Noble Dawn immediately. Any delay will only make matters worse.

He's putting his pack in the car when a man appears at the end of the driveway, a small man with shaggy, curly hair and a sharp nose. He wears shorts and boots; a few wood shavings cling to his jersey. His eyes gleam at Chris's late-model car.

'Gidday, mate.'

'Hey, how's it going?'

'I'm Ritchie. Thought I'd say gidday. I'm just over the road at number 3. Staying long?'

Chris shakes his hand and introduces himself. 'I have to go back to Wellington for a bit.'

'You just got here, mate.'

'I know, mate. The annoying thing is that I just have to do one thing. Then I'll be straight back.'

'I guess the missus is a bit pissed off about that, mate. Saw her marching off.' He giggles.

'Yeah, she's pretty stressed. Needs some peace and quiet, mate.'

'Well, this is a good spot for that.'

'Yeah, peace and quiet, no one bothering her. That's what she needs.'

'Good stuff.'

'All right, Ritchie. I'll be off.'

'Drive safely.'

As soon as Ritchie disappears into his house Chris follows the trail Hitomi took into the pines. His footsteps are muffled and wind in the branches roars above him in deathly stillness. The roaring is the sea, he realises. At the top of the rise he sees it, a dull grey expanse collapsing on the long sandy beach. He scans the dark trunks around him, the beds of orange and brown needles, looking for a flash of blond. Nothing. But someone or something has been down the dune, leaving wide and shallow circular tracks. He steps onto the sand and sinks. After a few steps he looks back. His tracks are the same. He runs. The sand is heavy and in his haste to find her and save her he stumbles. He checks himself, lets his breathing settle. The wide and sandy beach is deserted in both directions. No harm will come to her here. It's only sand, sea, and a few gulls under a lead sky. His strange anxiety abates. 'Crazy bitch,' he mutters and follows the odd tracks at a sedate pace. Sensibly, they veer back toward the pines. He sees her sitting on a bone-smooth log in the shadowy eave of the trees. She doesn't wave and neither does he. Staring ahead, she frowns with her mouth as he sits on the log next to her.

'You did a good job with the clippers.'

'I've been cutting my own hair for years.'

'It felt very intimate for me to cut your hair. I know you were bored.'

'I've had a lot of haircuts, I suppose.'

'Huh.' She stands and walks into the pines.

'Hitomi, wait.'

Over her shoulder she calls, 'I know what you think of me.'

He follows. 'No. Listen to me. Stop. We need to talk.'

'You'll tell me I'm not crazy while thinking I'm getting crazier by the minute.'

'Wait.' He takes her by the arm and she flinches as if expecting a blow. He's surprised. Gently, he says, 'Hitomi, the neighbour saw you run into the pines. He thinks you're my wife.'

Expressionless, she says, 'That's funny.'

'I need to pick you up in the car somewhere and sneak you back to the house.'

'No. I can sneak back through the trees.'

'All right.' He releases her.

'You can go now.'

'All right.'

'Travel safely.' Her attempted smile is a brief grimace.

'How long will you stay?'

'Until I can arrange a lift. There's a phone in the house, right?'

'The neighbour is nosy. Keep the door locked and the curtains drawn.'

'I hope the dog in Auckland is nice.'

'I'm afraid he isn't.'

She blinks for more information.

'He had my niece murdered, and probably my brother's wife.'

'A Kiwi?'

'No.'

She looks down and nods. 'Good luck. Please remember me with affection.'

Suddenly emotional, he strides away, certain he'll never see her again. But by the time he's retraced his steps to the house he has changed his mind. Unlike the pines, stuck in one place and roaring their heads off, he is an agent capable of choice and making change. He drives to the shop and buys a box of food and supplies for her. His generosity pleases him, makes him feel good. It's right. This is who I am, he thinks.

When he returns, the door is wide open. It exasperates him that she should be so reckless, particularly after he warned her. He dumps the box of supplies in the kitchen and calls her name. Silence. His heart begins to bang. And then he sees that the bathroom door is closed and hears the beat of the shower. It feels like a lucky reprieve. He knocks and cracks open the door.

She's bald. Her face, made alarmingly expressive, widens in horror.

'What the—'

'Get out!' she shrieks.

He stands in shock outside the door. The water shuts off and he hears her sobbing. In the lounge he opens the bottle of wine he bought for her and sits at the table. He's on to his second glass when she appears, bewigged and meek. Although dressed warmly in her jacket and jeans, she looks cold.

She speaks in English. 'Did I appear miserable to you?'

'What happened?'

She looks down. 'Huh.'

'Glass of wine?'

'No, I'm allergic to alcohol. You know that.'

He hadn't known that, but remains silent.

'I think I'm crazy, yeah?'

'Why?'

'I . . . you'll be angry. Sorry. I apologise in advance at what I'm about to tell you. I was fired. I lied to you. I was fired for inappropriate behaviour. With a man. Not you, huh. That's all I want to say. You can go now.'

'I bought you some food. I'll come back in a few days to check if you're here.'

She blinks at him. Tears tangle in her eyelashes. In Japanese: 'This is why I'm so sensitive about questions of sanity. I keep doing things I know I shouldn't. I know full well the danger and irrationality of my actions, and the consequences of doing them.' She gestures to the door he closed. 'I left it open knowing I shouldn't. Would a rational person do that?'

'Did you want the neighbour to come in?'

'I made a wish that you'd come back.' She shrugs and a rueful smile flashes across her face.

'It worked.'

'Yes.'

'Who shaved your head?'

'It's a ritual humiliation.' She blushes beneath her wig but is angry as well. 'It's a ceremony performed in front of a group of people who were required to leave Japan. Some of them, most of them, for stupid little reasons, really. We're called Settlers, right.' She finds his eyes. 'You know.'

'Yes.'

'Have you always known?'

'Yes.'

She blushes deeply again. Then she's on his lap. So light. Unexpectedly, she buries her face into his neck. The sudden gesture of trust and surrender unnerves him a little.

'I love you,' she says.

'I think I must love you, too.'

She kisses him passionately on the mouth. Immediately excited, he carries her to the bedroom, kissing her all the way. As soon as he's torn off her clothes he laps her clit greedily and a thought comes to mind that he tries to repress regarding the clippers and her bush. He can't fight it. *I want to shave her pussy and fuck her all day.* She's pushing his head down, moaning, when he decides to go for it. He pulls on his trousers and T-shirt.

'Where are you going?'

'Back in a minute.'

Her response when he returns from the car with the clippers in hand surprises him. She spreads her legs, arches her back and twists one of her thick, tubular nipples. He fumbles with the plug as he pushes it into the socket. The buzz draws a groan from her. He puts the vibrating thing on the bed and strips. She's very wet.

'Just preparing you for your haircut, madam,' he says, while finger-fucking her. 'Have you had a good day?'

'Yes. I, uh . . .' She groans.

Her bush comes away thrillingly easily.

'Careful,' she tells him.

He works slowly. 'A little wider, madam. Beautiful. Hasn't the weather been mild? Is this okay?' he asks, resting the vibrating body of the clippers on her.

'Mmmm.' She bites her lip and pushes them away. 'I want you now,' she tells him.

He looks down and watches his cock pistoning in her naked pussy. She utters a guttural cry, unlike any sound she's made before, and he comes a few seconds later. The clippers buzz away as they lie together panting.

'Looks good,' he says, standing up to admire his handiwork.

'Like a little girl.'

'Not from here.'

She runs an experimental hand over it. 'Feels weird.'

While she's in the bathroom he digs the moisturiser out of his bag. What was supposed to be a quick, practical skincare procedure turns into a long and very localised massage. Although exhausted, he's fascinated by the smooth and silky sensation. Her pussy's been transformed, opened like a flower, and is all petals under his circling fingers. She rolls onto her stomach. 'Fuck me.' Under his nose the wig is annoying, a cold curtain of nylon, but he has no desire to remove it. He pulls her up onto all fours. Her head hangs between the peaks of her wide shoulders. The image of her shaved head flashes through his mind, the amplified expression of horror drawn on her face as if in heavy black lines. The dark stubbled skull. Cancer, death camps, impending death. Witches were shaved. A keening wail escapes from her, punctuated with each thrust. Beautiful women in league with the Devil. Recklessly fucking him. He sees her naked on a broomstick, sliding up and down it in front of a half-circle of mechanics in some little garage in Petone or Lower Hutt. It's an act against death, against life-numbing respectability. He fucks away the remains of the Kiwi Auto Parts manager, or whoever it was, who didn't fuck her like this: with her face down in the pillow, wailing, with her shaved pussy up in the air.

His body feels stretched and pummelled, as it does after a physical game well won. Fulfilled, at peace, he brings her tea and microwaved dumplings in bed. She sips and nibbles whereas he wolfs his dumplings down on his way back to the bedroom. His eyes droop as soon as he climbs into bed.

178

He hears a window open, the snap of her lighter. Then she's snuggling close. He speaks into the back of her wig.

'What did you do wrong in Japan?'

'A silly little thing.'

Rolling away from her is the only way of communicating his displeasure he can manage.

'I thought the society here might be freer. I was wrong.'

It's a true enough sounding claim, he thinks, and falls asleep.

# Chapter 22:

# Hunger and anger

It's gloomy when he wakes. She's asleep, turned away. An item-by-item procession of the food he bought for her floats through his mind, along with associated cooking times. On the other hand there are takeaways. Yes, he thinks, better not to eat all her food and then leave. After a shower he finds her still asleep. It's dark. He writes a note and self-consciously adds two Xs. The blue-black air outside is cold and enervating. A steady breeze sounds in the pines; the sea is loud and tasteable. It strikes him as a good time to stretch his legs before the long drive to Auckland later, but his hunger is disrupting his peace of mind. It's rare for him to be so hungry, to experience the discomfort many people deal with regularly: thought-destroying, ease-annihilating hunger. He checks the door has locked behind him. The kitchen light is only dimly visible through the heavy curtains in the lounge. She's secure.

He's salivating at the smell of fish and chips filling the car as he pulls up at the bach. The glazed figure of his brother gleams in the headlights in its spot under the apple tree. 'Don't worry, bro,' he tells it. 'After I eat, I'm going. I'll let Noble Dawn know that—' Out of the corner of his eye he sees something large disappear into the pines. He leaps out of the car and sees the tops of a couple of young trees shiver. They're only fifty metres away but pursuit would be hopeless without a torch. *Ritchie.* He's probably standing there panting, looking at him now, the nosy little prick. Chris is about to sprint for the pines, if only to work off his rising fury, when he sees the lights on at Ritchie's house, where Ritchie, he knows, is not home. He decides to ask Ritchie's wife what he was doing in their backyard. First, he takes the fish and chips from the car. Hitomi opens the door and welcomes him with a smile of unusual warmth, a beautiful smile. She's wrapped in a towel and is still wet from a shower. It erases any doubt in his mind as to what has happened: Ritchie's been looking in the bathroom window.

'Be right back. Close the door.'

You pervy little bastard, he thinks as he marches across the road. At the letterbox he pauses, thinking Ritchie may flush himself from hiding rather than have the issue taken inside his house. He waits for a while, scanning the pines, and becomes aware of the sound of trickling water, the hollow rattle that occurs when a sink is drained or a shower used. He walks up a few steps and looks up the side of the house: a narrow path overhung with bush. A light is on, a top window cracked open; the fragile breath of steam passes into darkness. The vantage point, should he wish to look in the bathroom window, is on top of the retaining wall.

He knocks loudly on the back door, only two windows down from the shower. Water continues to run in the drain. He knocks again. The water continues. What he wants, before he dies of hunger, is to ascertain whether it's Ritchie in the shower. If it is, he can go and eat. Quickly, he heaves himself up onto the wall and crawls along it through brushing pungent ferns and ponga. It's a woman's face, lulled near unconsciousness; her eyes are closed, her dark wet hair slicked back. He's about to let himself down off the wall when he hears footsteps. After a moment's deliberation he sits back deep in the ferns. It's not Ritchie but a large bearded man of about fifty, swinging a chilly bin. Under his bush shirt is a pronounced beer gut. He seems to test the door. It's unlocked and he lets himself in. Chris jumps down off the wall, brushes the soil off his pants and jacket, and knocks. The shower continues. He knocks again.

'Yeah?' The bearded man regards him with open suspicion.

'Gidday mate. Is Ritchie around?'

'Who?'

'Ritchie. He said he lives here.'

'Never heard of him.'

'This tall, curly hair. About forty. Shorts and boots.'

'Never seen him before.'

'He came over this morning. Said he lives here in number 3.'

'All kinds of dodgy buggers hang around here off-season, mate.'

'Okay. Thanks.'

He heads for the beach with the vague hope of stumbling across Ritchie by chance, but as soon as he takes the path at the end of the cul-de-sac into the pines it becomes apparent that it's very unlikely to happen. It seems an army could hide there. Still, he persists along the track. The rising wind announces itself in the branches overhead and something cracks. The ocean thumps and roars. He hurries back.

Her welcoming smile is less radiant this time.

Seeing the unopened packet on the table he cries, 'You haven't started yet?' He tears it open and upends the little pottle of tomato sauce. After a piece of fish he says, 'Something funny is going on next door.'

182

'Really?'

'Something strange. The guy I met this morning, Ritchie, the neighbour who I described as nosy, doesn't actually live over the road. The real neighbour has never heard of this Ritchie. Said he's probably just prowling around looking for something to steal.'

'Okay. Better keep the door shut, then.'

Her attitude strikes him as sensible. Ritchie, a sad little bloke, presents no danger if they take basic precautions. Her disapproval of the meal doesn't register until he's into his third piece of fish. She's picking, wiping her fingers clean on a napkin between chips.

'I'm glad you like it,' she says.

'I was starving.'

'This . . . sorry, I'd need to be starving to enjoy this. It's very greasy and tasteless.'

'And hot and filling.'

'Do they have bento or yakitori over there?'

'No, it's not for tourists.'

'Hmm.'

'Maybe you need to grow up with this food.'

'I think so.' She watches him eat, resentfully, it seems to him. 'But Kiwis like Japanese food too, not just tourists.'

'That's true. It's just a small traditional place. Quick and cheap.'

'The traditional food isn't good. Always deep fried, right? Like this.'

'Fish, yes. We used to eat a lot of beef and lamb, too.'

'A country surrounded by sea and it deep-fries its fish. I think it says something.'

'Really? What?'

She wipes her fingers on her napkin again. Like a fly, he thinks.

'It says we had a British heritage,' he tells her. 'We mainly

183

ate beef and lamb. Used to, anyway. Most of it goes to Japan now, or Ireland.'

'It's good to eat fish, if it's well prepared.'

'Well, tourists come here to eat beef. New Hokkaido, right?'

'Huh.' She pulls a face. 'It's not like real Hokkaido beef.' She wrinkles her nose over the remains of the chips and sauce on the greasy newspaper.

A phrase he has wanted to say many times over the years to a Japanese person comes to mind. For the first time in his life he actually says it. 'If you don't like the food here, go back to Japan.'

Her expression is cold and imperious. 'Your culture has no cuisine.'

He hears an echo in her phrase, perhaps an echo of some senior manager at Mazda. 'My favourite meal is roast lamb,' he tells her, 'with roast potatoes, pumpkin and kumara. With mint sauce, rosemary, gravy, salt and garlic.' In actual fact his favourite meal is sashimi, but he's furious, and is arguing with senior Japanese management, for once, as much as with her. 'It's a pity all the lamb goes overseas now. It's a pity New Zealand children don't get to taste it.'

'It's a barbaric meal.'

'Barbaric?' He laughs hollowly. 'Barbaric,' he repeats, violently scrunching the newspaper. 'When the word *barbaric* is used in this country, it's not usually in reference to roast lamb.'

'You know full well that Japanese cuisine is well regarded by your countrymen, especially by the younger generation who don't consider eating rice a political act.'

'It's always the last resort of pro-occupationists to say the food's better.' He gets up with the paper and walks to the kitchen.

She's apoplectic, unable to speak. Finally, it comes: 'Are

you saying you're anti-occupationist? Please tell me you're anti-occupationist?' Her goading tone is awful. She's daring him to say it, like a policeman looking for a chance to arrest him and beat him up.

'New Zealand is being run into the ground.'

'Say you're anti-occupationist.'

It's a line in the sand for her, he sees, so he steps back. 'Of course I'm grateful for the guidance of the IJA—it's a great privilege to be part of the Empire. But modernisation would have occurred here anyway. We were a first-world country in 1942. In fact, modernisation would have occurred at a faster rate without intervention. We'd be more than a New Hokkaido.'

'Much less, I think, from what I've seen.' She stares at him as if he's an insect.

'I'm anti-occupation,' he says, deliberately mildly.

'I must leave.'

He calls after her as she heads for the bedroom: 'That doesn't mean I'm anti-Japanese.'

'Huh.'

He stamps on the kitchen bin's pedal, sending the lid up with a bang, and throws the ball of newspaper hard. He misses. A familiar eye stares out of the ball of newsprint. It can't be, he thinks, teasing the paper open. It is; it's Patrick, with his hair in a topknot and wearing a kimono. Flattening the page on the bench, feeling guilty that he's still not on the road, he reads the caption. *Patrick Ipswitch, Rising Dragon, aka the Night Train, the New Zealand born Pan-Asian Sumo Champion, pictured above in 1982, has been charged with the murder of his mistress one week after the unsolved murder of their illegitimate child.*

Hitomi comes out of the bedroom in her jacket, eyes rigidly ahead as she heads for the door.

'See you,' he says, returning to the photo.

She slams the door and her footsteps quickly recede.

'A cracker in the end, after all that,' he tells the door. The sadness he hears in his voice, rather than the contempt he had intended, unnerves him. He's sorry for himself. For the first time he doubts he will be able to speak to Noble Dawn. Patrick's prosecution and almost certain death fill him with sorrow, and he fears being alone, of beginning a long and dreary struggle without end. He pours himself a glass of wine and shortly after pours another. He pictures Hitomi striding along the road in her blond wig, nose in the air, his sperm inside her. 'Anti-Japanese,' he says to himself. 'Jesus.' It's almost funny. He drains the bottle and goes outside for a cigarette. Headlights flare on the pines. Their phantom remains drift for a moment in darkness. From the end of the driveway he sees that a Toyota has pulled up at number 3. Ritchie gets out, still in his shorts and boots, and waves.

'Hey mate. You're back.'

Chris swiftly crosses the road. 'Ritchie?'

'Uh, yeah.'

'You said you live there at number 3?'

'Yeah. What's up?'

'But I just went over to see you and the guy in there doesn't know you.'

'Um, what? You been drinking?'

'No, yeah, just a wine with dinner. Listen, a big guy with a beard said he didn't know you.' He points. 'He was in your house.'

'Huh?' Ritchie turns and walks quickly up the steps. Chris follows. The drain is still gargling, the bathroom light still on and the top window cracked open, but there's no steam. A horrible premonition of death grips Chris as Ritchie opens the door in a proprietary way.

'Molly? Molly?' The calls become fainter as he goes further into the house.

186

In a moment of dazzling clarity, Chris sees everything. The big chilly bin the man carried contained a circular saw and bags. It's a frame-up: they want to frame him for this woman's murder. *Molly*'s murder. As the image returns of her blissfully closed eyes in the steam, he turns and runs. He gets into his car and tears away with the lights off to hide his number plates.

Approaching the intersection with the main road, with its phone box and fish-and-chip shop, he turns the lights on and a figure rears up before him. He swerves, just missing Hitomi, who is walking on the dark shoulder of the road. He stops in front of her and throws open the passenger door.

'Get in!'

She keeps walking.

He drives alongside her at walking pace. 'Please get in, Miss Kurosawa. Something's happened next door. I think there's been a murder.'

'Are you insane?'

The anger in her face is too much for him to overcome. He pulls the door closed and accelerates away.

# Chapter 23:

# A pie in Palmerston North

He drives fast to Palmerston North and buys a ticket for the late train to Auckland, which is due in thirty minutes. The timing is fortunate. His car has surely become a liability: Ritchie has seen it and the police will be looking for it. The long-term prospects are frightening so he refuses to consider what he'll do about the car after seeing Noble Dawn, if it's even at the station when he returns. He eats a pie to ease his anxiety. There's a phone box and he has time to kill. He tries a four-digit number from memory.

'Yes?'

'Hitomi.'

'Oh, what a surprise. Where are you?'

'Up the road a bit. Is everything okay?'

'I was very offended. You understand that I must be offended if you tell me that you hate my countrymen.'

'I don't hate them. I'd love to go to Japan. I just want self-rule for New Zealand.'

'I understand that.'

'You do?'

'Yes, very well.'

'Then what were we arguing about?'

'I cooked something. Are you hungry?'

'I just had a pie.'

'A pie.'

'It was amazing.'

'Huh.'

He fancies he can hear her smiling. 'I remembered the number,' he says, grateful for the connection it has enabled. 'It was written on the phone at the bach.'

'Four numbers. Oh, you did very well.'

'Did the police turn up over the road?'

'No.'

'Are you sure?'

'Wait . . . yes, it's quiet, no police.'

'I'm going. Please remember me kindly.'

'You can pick me up on your way back from Auckland if you like. I'd like to meet your new dog.'

'I'll call you.'

He's still smiling a minute after putting the phone down. It looks like the bearded man at Ritchie's was taking the piss, giving him—an obvious townie—the run-around. He goes to collect a refund on his train ticket but is told it's not possible. Even this can't dent his good mood, and after giving the ticket to a man approaching the window he feels even better.

Inside his car, his beautiful car, he puts on Johnny Lennon's banned *Rising Moon* album, turns it up loud and heads north. Not for the first time, he wishes Johnny were still alive. He's too young to remember Johnny's death, but Patrick told him a lot of people thought he was a loudmouth who brought it on himself, that his death was inevitable, and even that his homecoming gig in Levin was an act of suicide, since he was banned from public appearance, let alone public performance. And yet some people accused him of selling out. He was too abrasive, too naive, pro-Japanese, an anarchist, a clown, a drunk, a wife-beater, a criminal, a Maori-lover. To Chris he was a genius and everything he said or did was special, and if he contradicted himself when he was alive it was because he had to in order to please different factions. The fact that he made it to thirty-two is remarkable, given that he was such a lightning rod. But there is never anything ambiguous in the music; it is searingly truthful in the ways that really matter. Chris plays the track 'Pieces' three times in a row, singing along with gusto, and is filled with righteous passion. This music will last forever. In the end, Johnny believed in the humanity of all, Japanese included; and Chris, inspired and uplifted by Johnny as he so often is, believes in the humanity of Noble Dawn.

# Chapter 24:

# Auckland

When he finally gets onto the motorway south of Auckland, Chris feels he's made it, but the length and breadth of the road surprises him. He must have slept on the way in and out of the city on the trip with The Typhoons two years ago. It's early, only 5 am, and yet traffic is starting to flow. More than a million Japanese live here now. Down the highway, the city's dark towers have come into view, sprinkled with lights. They are both attractive and intimidating. A move to Auckland, away from his apartment and the familiar faces and streets of Wellington, would stretch him, but it feels inevitable that one day he will try his luck in the nation's major city. By comparison, Wellington is a village of shabby three-storeyed poured concrete boxes. It's an administrative centre and a transport hub, but there's no real money around, and the reason he stays is because he grew up and played rugby there. He knows Wellington's rules. It feels like the towers of Auckland looming higher down the motorway would make him or break him in ways he can only guess at.

He knows Karangahape Road and Ponsanabe from the rugby trip, so he heads there. The day labourers are leaving their guesthouses as he arrives. Like ghosts or smoking sleepwalkers, they wait for the trams that will take them to the wharf at the bottom of Empress Street.

He wants something a little more upmarket than a working man's house. In Ponsanabe he finds a bed-and-breakfast, a large wooden bungalow advertising a vacancy and parking at the rear. It reminds him of the guesthouse his mother ran. A good omen. He pulls on the handbrake in the leafy car park with satisfaction.

The asking price is more than he expected. The Kiwi receptionist, a grandmotherly type, sees him blanch at the cost and offers to throw in a free breakfast. The smell of bacon wafting out of the dining room makes his mind up. After dropping his bag in a double room glowing with polished kauri, he eats his fill and drinks coffee over the paper. The fifteen-day sumo tournament has already started. Some of the celebrity judges for the senior bouts are listed, but Noble Dawn's retirement name is different again from his fighting and birth names, and Chris has forgotten it. Even if he's not a judge, Chris is certain he will be there, that the tournament is the reason he came to New Zealand. He's sure that the revenge was not plotted from afar but opportunistic, that when Noble Dawn got to New Zealand and saw that Patrick was isolated he spontaneously decided to settle an old score. Noble Dawn was an athlete, and that's how athletes are. They see, they fight, they forget. Until they see again. Regarding the missing Lyttelton Ferry, Chris sees there are no further developments. It is assumed the boat sank rapidly in deep water near Kaikoura.

The sky is lightening as he heads out on foot to secure a ticket for the tournament from the booking office on Empress Street. As he walks he thinks through the apology he will present on his brother's behalf. He practised it in the car on the drive up, this earnest and deeply felt apology,

192

but the words are still somewhat vague given that he has no idea what Patrick did to earn Noble Dawn's wrath. He stops at a phone box and tries the prison. No luck. For a moment he considers calling Hitomi. I know what she did, he thinks: she fucked around and didn't respect institutions. 'An honorary Kiwi,' he says to himself, and leaves the phone on the hook.

The Japanese woman in the ticket office regards his request with suspicion. He knows there's no way he can get a seat near the front and will have to sit at the back in the ghetto reserved for Kiwi sumo enthusiasts. Even so, the ticket is expensive.

'Sorry, is one of the judges the esteemed wrestler previously known as Noble Dawn?'

'Pardon me, I don't know that name.' A phone call confirms that he is.

Is this the key, he thinks, a lack of fame compared to Patrick?

Empress Street at rush hour is too much for him in his fragile, sleepless state. Too many coffees have made him seedy. There are way too many people and almost all are Japanese. A homeless local is bowed in a doorway. A tram clangs past and he sees more of his countrymen: hungover labourers making their way, late, to the wharfs in the hope of a miracle. The magazine shop he enters feels like a place of refuge. Far from the door he finds the current issue of *Sumo* and several back issues. The current names mean nothing to him, but he recognises the profiles of great wrestlers of the past and their statistics are familiar to him. He reads the experts' opinions as to how they would fare today. Like most New Zealanders, his enjoyment of sumo ended with the Night Train's retirement and the subsequent failure of another Kiwi to reach the first division. It was a strange, short-lived national passion. Commentators said he won many of his fights before contact, and it was true that even lay people watching at home saw that many of his opponents were visibly disconcerted by his gaze. Chris, like everyone else, knew where that gaze came from. After the charge would come the Night Train's trademark flurry of open-handed blows at the throat and chest of his opponent. From there the bout could go anywhere: trips, pushes, lift-outs. As supreme champion, wearing the heavy rope around his waist, the nation cheered when he swung his legs high and crashed them down on the ring, clearing it of evil spirits. He was as big as anyone in the competition and explosively fast. The gaze that rattled opponents said: *This sacred ring is my country and I'm clearing you out of it.*

Chris puts the last sumo magazine down. In his mind he's been over his meeting with Noble Dawn at Patrick's house several times, and now he does it again. The man was blunt with Chiyo in a way that suggested familiarity. More than just accepting him and his bluntness, she appeared grateful, probably because he'd broken the drought of celebrity visitors. He checks himself. Only Chiyo could tell him the truth about that, and she has gone. He hasn't given much thought to her disappearance and feels guilty about it. Only occasionally does he even consider her dead, but now is one of those times. What gets him is the love his brother has lost. They were good together. She was good for him. It was a big, inconvenient love that took courage. And Sarah was the pure living proof of the rightness of it. Weary of standing, feeling he might weep, he joins the bustle of Empress Street again.

# Chapter 25:

## The sumo tournament

From his entry point high in the arena, he sees Noble Dawn seated in the senior north judge's position on the edge of the platform. The other four judges, obviously ex-wrestlers, have lost weight in retirement; only Noble Dawn has ballooned. The hair slicked back on his motionless head lacks only the fan-shaped topknot of an active wrestler, whereas the others wear civilian hairstyles. It's 4 pm, the senior bouts in the first class division are underway, and the 15,000-person stadium is at full capacity. It would only hold 10,000 Kiwis, he thinks, spreading out on the bench seats in the way Japanese consider slovenly. A short separate bench is above the main octagonal arena, with only a handful of Kiwis on it. The last time he was here he was fourteen; Patrick was fighting, and he watched with his mother from the inner ring in a box seat that no amount of money could buy. The Kiwi fans, all men, stare at him as he sits down.

'Jeez mate, you're like a skinny young version of the Night Train.'

'My bro.'

They stand and nod their heads in the unique Kiwi semi-bow, shake his hand and slap his shoulder. They tell him his brother was the greatest and they're sorry for what's happened. It's an unusual reaction but it feels right. The rest of the country's crazy, he thinks. Politely, conversation turns to the quality of the view despite the distance from the ring, and as the preparations for the next bout begin the fans refer to their programmes and mark them with pens.

Both senior wrestlers in the next bout are seen as potential Junior Champions, the fans tell him, although one is significantly smaller than the other. As is usually the case, Chris finds himself rooting for the smaller man as the rituals begin. The men throw salt, then they squat opposite each other, break and stand simultaneously, rinse their mouths in the corner, throw more salt. Squat; break. Upon entering the ring for the third time, the larger man throws a great emphatic spray of salt and the crowd starts to buzz. The wrestlers squat. The glare this time is serious. The larger man's hand goes down, makes contact with the ring: he's ready. The smaller man touches the ring, and they charge. After the slap of impact the smaller man burrows in, trying for a belt hold, but the larger man gets under the smaller, stands him up briefly and forks his throat with a meaty hand. The smaller man slides back, pushed by his throat, until his back foot hits the edge of the ring. He braces both feet on the raised circle, but the larger man still has him by the throat. He is being lifted by the throat from the ring when he somehow frees his head and turns away in one swift and supple movement. Suddenly having nothing to push against, the larger man's momentum carries him out of the ring, headfirst off the platform and into the front seats. The dramatic reversal brings the crowd to its feet, but the ring referee rules that the smaller wrestler's foot touched the ground outside the ring before the other man's body. The crowd boos. They begin stamping. Noble Dawn climbs to his feet, throws a pinch of salt, and enters the ring with the other judges. Standing in the centre, he frowns and folds his mighty arms. The other judges surround him, remonstrating, throwing their hands in the air in exasperation. More boos and jeering, growing louder and louder. Cushions sail into the ring. Finally, Noble Dawn unfolds his arms and nods. The ring referee's decision is overturned. The smaller wrestler is declared the winner. The crowd's jeers turn to cheers, and Chris joins the other Kiwis on their feet clapping.

He asks the fan next to him, 'What do you know about Noble Dawn?'

'Well, his highest ranking was only Senior Wrestler in the First Class, but he had a knack of beating your brother, I'm sorry to say. No other wrestler beat the Night Train more.'

'What was his secret?'

'That was much pondered upon. He just seemed to have the wood on him.'

The fans discuss the forthcoming bout and are knowledgeable about both wrestlers. Chris consults his programme. Recognising none of the names, he says he's looking forward to the Mongolians and the Bulgarian. Although the fans smile and nod he can tell they're disappointed; they're connoisseurs who appreciate technique and a good bout, regardless of nationality. It occurs to Chris that this is the first tournament he's watched without his brother competing. He was never a genuine fan of the sport like these guys are; there was too much at stake on a personal level. He finds he's more patient now and enjoys the showmanship in the rituals preceding the fights in a way that he didn't as a boy.

After a long bout in which the advantage swaps twice, a wrestler is hoisted by his belt clear off the ground and carried from the ring. While in the air he briefly waves his legs, and

Chris sees that the helpless gesture is for theatrical effect. The fight was sincere, but that brief comical waggle—when the bout was effectively lost—was for the crowd. It's something his brother would never have done. For him, sumo was not about entertainment, although his determination and will to win quickly and violently were tremendously entertaining. The Night Train: his popular name suited him. The Japanese loved to hate him. And plain hated him, too, apparently.

As the bouts continue and more beer and sake are consumed, the crowd become more vocal. 'He's got no chance!' 'Forget it!' 'Go for it!' 'Go, go, go!' Chris begins to see the wrestlers as a fraternity, a band of brothers at the centre of a storm. They are gladiators bound for an early death due to heart disease and liver failure; a noble group of warriors which the Night Train relentlessly ran through, again and again, for fifteen years. The apology to Noble Dawn that has been brewing in Chris's mind changes form.

When a new group of judges come in, Noble Dawn stands and waddles, stiff-armed, for the exit. In a flash Chris is on the concourse under the stadium seating, waiting outside the entrance to the VIP area. Three old men in new suits come out with cigarettes in their mouths, rummaging in their pockets. Chris steps up and offers the flame of his lighter. It is ignored. They move away, rummage a little longer and produce one of their own. After a couple of puffs, he is noticed.

'Young man, you look familiar.'

Chris bows low. 'Thank you for saying so, sir. I am hoping to pay tribute to my brother's greatest opponent, the honourable Noble Dawn.'

'Ahhh.'

'You didn't take up the sport?'

'My mother wouldn't allow it.'

They smile at this and he feels he is being considered

for something, a job perhaps. Great opportunity is theirs to give, but no further question or comment comes. In fact they're just smoking together, he realises, and he happens to be close enough, two metres away, to sense their aura of privilege and power.

The VIP door cracks open and a disappointingly slim man comes out.

One of the three men stubs his cigarette out half-finished and returns through the door. The dialogue is over. Uncomfortable at the silence Chris feels he is imposing, he chooses a more distant ashtray to smoke by.

'Wait.'

'Yes, sir.'

The man who left, the junior at sixty-ish, returns with a twinkle in his eyes. He speaks to his companions loudly enough for Chris to overhear.

'Noble Dawn has been kind enough to agree to smoke with us.'

'Oh dear, what does he smoke? I have only local cigarettes.'

'Aha.' One of them holds up a pack of Cut Silk.

'Excellent. We don't want him grumpy.'

'No.'

'The Night Train versus the Castle,' says the sleekest of the three fondly. 'Irresistible force meets irresistible object.'

'No doubt the Night Train had the better of his opponent,' says one of the men ruefully.

'Yes.'

Chris takes his cue. 'Pardon me for saying so, honoured gentlemen, but Noble Dawn proved more than my brother's equal in the ring.'

His words have the desired effect, the men are pleased, but their smiles make him suspect he's missing something; probably they find his respectful speech amusing. Masuda always says his more formal language is too flowery, like a greeting card.

'I loved their fights,' says one of the old men with sudden boyish enthusiasm.

Chris bows to express his gratitude. It's going far better than he could have hoped and it is time for him to be silent.

Another slim person exits the VIP door.

'Tokyo, the first tournament of the season, '79 or '80. It was magnificent. A minute in and the crowd were on their feet. And still it went on. Noble Dawn produced an outer arm throw: the first and last I ever saw from him!'

'Yes!'

'Yes!'

Chris remembers. Noble Dawn was lower ranked and expected to lose. He remembers the uncharacteristic curses and groans from the boarders—even Nadine, the typist—as they watched the bout late at night in the lounge together, the blankets falling to the floor as everyone stood before the television and the bout went on and on.

'Perhaps the young gentleman has a different recollection?'

He's watched it several times on video since. It became a glorious loss in New Zealand, being the last bout in a gruelling tournament, in which a relative unknown, buoyed by the crowd, produced a superhuman effort to win. Superhuman strength was required to beat the Night Train in those days.

'You've described the winning throw as I remember it,' Chris says. 'It was executed with such authority that I'm surprised to learn it was not a stock technique of Noble Dawn's.'

The VIP door cracks open to reveal a white-gloved attendant, who steps through and hold the door wide. Noble Dawn fills the frame and then projects himself through it.

'The Castle,' says one of the old men, to alert Noble Dawn to their presence as much as anything.

'More like the Wall these days,' he replies.

The men laugh. The one with Japanese cigarettes offers up his packet. With his great sausage fingers the wrestler picks one, as if it were a toothpick. Chris knows he will not be noticed until he's introduced so he waits quietly, eyes averted.

'You were faced with a difficult decision. It must be hard to concentrate when the cushions are flying.'

The old men laugh, but Noble Dawn merely creases his eyes. His popular name, the Castle, suits him; he is serious and forbidding. Chris suspects that his line about becoming the Wall is used frequently.

'Still, I suppose cushions in the ring are as bad as it gets these days,' offers the sleekest of the old men. 'In fact, speaking of as bad as it gets, you might remember Rising Dragon, AKA the Night Train; his younger brother is here to pay his respects.'

Noble Dawn swivels his head like the turret of a battleship.

'Sorry, forgive me, sir.' Chris bows low and looks down. 'I was not myself when you visited my brother's house. I have come to offer my gratitude for your great kindness and consideration.'

'This brings you to Auckland?' The question is sharp.

'Well, um, not entirely. Business, sir. This opportunity came up—'

'He looks like his brother.'

'Maybe too much,' says Noble Dawn.

The older men erupt with laughter at this.

'Sorry,' Chris says, and there is more laughter. Noble Dawn seems baffled. He stands there, grown too big for even his custom-made jacket. The buttons will never be done up. He takes a final puff and lobs the un-stubbed cigarette at the ashtray.

'Please come to dinner tonight after the tournament. All

of you. You too, Little Train. At Ozeki in Empress Street.'

Chris, holding a low bow, hears the pleasure in the old men's voices as they accept the invitation. He maintains his bow until they have all returned through the VIP door, then he walks straight out of the stadium and offers his thanks to the night sky.

# Chapter 26:

# Deadly dinner

Back at the plush guesthouse Chris takes a long shower in his private bathroom. It has a large claw-foot bath as well and room for half a dozen more besides. All the fine-grained glowing wood makes him suspect it was once a double bedroom. So many sleepers have lain here, he thinks; so many others have prepared to go out. It makes him feel both less alone and more miserable. He lathers up for a shave and as he makes the first stroke he begins his apology, which he intends to deliver as late as possible, the later the better, as the murderer will be made more amenable by drink, food, and good company. 'Before my brother departs this world,' he tells the mirror, 'he wants to make amends with all those he has wronged.' It's fair to expect such a comment will go unchallenged, he thinks as he continues to shave; or perhaps there will be an objection along the lines of *it's too late for apologies now*. Either way, he'll follow up with: 'Although it's too late for him to repair the damage he caused in this world, he would like to pass on to the next knowing he has left no ill-feeling amongst those he respected most. He feels this particularly strongly concerning you, Noble

Dawn, his greatest opponent.' Surely the man will listen, Chris thinks as he rinses his face with cold water. His face is revealed to him in the mirror, clear and open. Perhaps such a moment of clarity will occur in the apology, when Noble Dawn will see the man standing before him and recognise the humanity of the man who did him wrong. 'Although my brother won many bouts, he realises he had no real success.' He rests his hands on the sink and observes his eyes in the mirror. The apology is not watertight. Was it the code of the warrior that Patrick violated, or was it something intensely and horribly personal? The black points from which he sees, centred in brown disks flecked with green, give nothing back. His brother's authority was always benevolent and genial. Only in the ring did he coldly hate. 'My brother regrets many things, but his unworthy hatred he regrets most of all. No . . . my brother recognises the justice of his impending death. And asks that you forgive him his—immaturity . . .' For the first time Chris doubts himself and the power of apology and forgiveness in an honourable world. 'Oh, my brother asks that you . . . ah . . . agree to a re-match. Ah!' He stretches, throws a few lazy punches and a quick combination: one-two-three. 'He is thankful that his death will release him from the rage that has consumed him.' Picturing his dead niece—a bundle of rags stuffed under a hedge—he throws more punches. The bathroom is a boxing ring; the towel around his waist is his trunks. He throws long punishing jabs at Noble Dawn's basketball-sized head. The wrestler is blowing air already and baffled. 'He asks that you be amongst those who execute him for his wife's murder. And that you dig her up from wherever you buried her.' He's ducking, moving side to side; the lumbering giant is cut and bleeding into his right eye. Two minutes left in the round. One-two-three-four: a vicious combination. 'My brother says sorry.' Chris's eyes are full too. He blinks, wipes them, and continues to jab. 'Sorry for being invaded. Sorry for speaking English. Sorry for frying fish. Sorry for queuing badly.' One-two-three. 'Sorry for getting rheumatic fever. Sorry for being malnourished.' Left hook, right cross. 'Sorry for making a noise, for being too big, for not concentrating, sorry, sorry, sorry.' One-two-three. 'For not being Japanese.' Right cross. 'Whatever my brother did, he's fucked now. Are you happy? Ah.' He stops and shakes himself. At the mirror again he tries to find his brother's soul in his own eyes. 'My brother . . . my brother . . .' There's nothing. Patrick gets angry sometimes, but not crazy angry. He was a mischievous kid, by all accounts, a practical joker who grew into a generous man who cared for his family and married for love. He didn't fuck around in the ring, that's all. There are beads of perspiration on Chris's face. He showers again quickly in cooler water, applies deodorant and aftershave, puts on a clean white shirt and tie. 'I'll do my best,' he tells his reflection in Japanese.

It's early so he walks from Ponsanabe to Empress Street and sits in the window of a small bar opposite the restaurant and waits for Noble Dawn's party to arrive. Food is likely to be the number one priority for the big man after the tournament, so he doesn't expect to wait long. Indeed, halfway through his first beer, a limousine pulls up to great fanfare from the parking attendants as Noble Dawn, his personal attendant, and two of the judges climb out. Another chauffeur-driven car pulls up, a Cadillac by the look of it, and more men climb out, including two of the older men he met at the VIP door. It's an impressive arrival: a display of power, money and flesh that stops the foot-traffic. Attempting to ignore a burst of nerves, he drains his beer and stands up.

When he enters the reception area, with its leather couches and aquarium-like tanks full of live produce, the head waiter waves him away. In English: 'Full.'

'Sorry. I've been invited to join the sumo wrestler's party.'

The man's eyes widen.

'The Castle; Noble Dawn; the ex-sumo wrestler.'

'One moment.'

A waiter is dispatched behind the screens which shield the restaurant proper from view and protect the diners' privacy from the street. It's a celebrity eatery. While Chris waits he looks at the fish, lobster and crabs in the scrupulously clean holding tanks. *A great honour*, he says to himself. *My brother always spoke of you with the greatest respect.* Time passes. He has looked in all the tanks and now begins a second round. The light is deep green and purple; the bubbles aerating the water are plentiful and pretty. Five-star accommodation for those on death row. It's one of the best restaurants in the country, probably the best. The filthy, brightly lit tanks filled with floaters and barely stirring creatures along the waterfront at Island Bay in Wellington come to mind. Still the waiter hasn't returned. The black-eyed creatures are beginning to depress him despite the exquisite lighting, so he sits on a couch. The young shoe attendants, Kiwis, are nervous. Standing to attention at each end of the shoe shelf, they flick their eyes over him. 'Evening, boys,' he says quietly in English. They glance at each other and smile. More diners arrive and the boys set to work, placing the shoes in the shelf corresponding to the guests' table. Not until more than fifteen minutes have elapsed does the head waiter beckon to him. The restaurant is dim. There are no single tables, only long low ones on tatami mats widely spaced to allow the deployment of screens, should they be required. The far wall is dominated by large and permanent screens painted with images of a Japanese coast, its tidy arrangement of drowned rocky hills and bonsai-like trees, so unlike anything in New Zealand. He follows the waiter through these to the VIP section, the longest table of all, seating thirty-odd diners, at which Noble Dawn sits at the head like a boulder. Cigars are being smoked as the day's bouts are discussed. The diners are all men, and in such a strictly hierarchical situation Chris knows he is the lowest of the low. He is thankful to see a space at the bottom corner, even though it's as far from Noble Dawn as it's possible to be. There is no cushion for him. Chris bows, and as soon as the waiter has taken his jacket, he bows lower, apologises, and takes his place quickly and quietly. He is not noticed by the table, but those next to him, wealthy men who are ten years older than he, flick their eyes over him. One of them grunts his displeasure. The waiter fills his glass with hot sake, which will be his last drink at the table, he guesses, because no other guest is likely to pour for him. The appetiser set before him is a brown jelly topped with what appears to be skin. It tastes smoky. It's five-star food and he pays attention. The dish is a nice combination of soft and chewy, but nothing special.

'Fugu,' says the man next to him.

Chris's reaction, an almost unconscious Japanese-style expression of exaggerated wide-eyed shock, draws a chuckle from the speaker. Chris is, in fact, genuinely shocked. The poisonous pufferfish is fatal if not prepared correctly, and only served legally at qualified restaurants of the most expensive and exclusive kind. Yet despite these precautions, there are fatalities every year. It's his first taste. He focuses on his lips and tongue, anticipating the sensation of numbness that announces a fatal dose of poison and the untreatable onset of paralysis. It doesn't come. He takes the whole glass of sake at one shot. There's another laugh.

Noble Dawn announces: 'At the end, we have the Night Train's little brother.'

The *Aaaah*s emitted are of relief as much as anything; his presence now makes some sense. His neighbour tops up his glass. Bowing, Chris says, 'Thank you, sir, for this great honour. My brother always spoke of you in the highest possible terms.'

Noble Dawn says into the silence, 'The praise of one great man is worth the censure of many common ones.'

There is uncertain laughter.

'You are too generous, sir,' Chris says as meekly as he can while remaining audible.

'The Night Train can't be here, so you must eat in his place,' says Noble Dawn. 'We will eat fugu. Eat like it's your last meal.'

It's a toast the table embraces. Glasses are raised but Chris dares not raise his. He sips humbly instead. Conversation breaks out, wrestling talk, and the tension created by his arrival dissipates. Those at the other end of the table, the most senior of the party and the most important, can speak freely as long as they speak quietly. The sake kicks in. He'd like to loosen his tie but it's too soon for such a familiar gesture. The path for his apology must be cleared diligently. The next dish is a stew in which the fugu is noticeable as a texture among the vegetables and broth rather than a taste. Again he checks for a creeping numbness, a tingling, in his mouth and lips.

The mention of the Night Train at the other end of the table sharpens his ears. The speaker is one of the judges, an ex-wrestler who looks about the same age as Patrick and Noble Dawn. 'It's murder. Not completely surprising considering his history. I hear he's been taken in for beating up women in the past.'

Chris feels his face flush and busies himself with his chopsticks. On an empty stomach, the sake has him reeling.

'Yes, he was arrested in Japan too,' says Noble Dawn loudly, to expressions of surprise. 'But it was hushed up.'

'Arrested?'

'For fighting in Fukuoka. More than once. He was a great favourite of the Yakuza of course. That's why he got away with what he did.'

One of the older men he met previously at the VIP door speaks up. 'It's odd that the Yakuza would favour a foreigner given their rabid nationalist sentiments.'

An unknown voice. 'Come on. They're all Koreans!'

The table laughs at length.

'He beat up a woman?'

'On more than one occasion, I heard.'

'But *murder*? Is this in keeping with his character?'

Noble Dawn wipes perspiration from his forehead with a napkin and regards the other judges, the two ex-wrestlers, but remains silent.

'Well,' says the first judge, 'I don't mind being carried out of the ring by my belt—yes, it happened once or twice—but I don't like being unnecessarily upended on the way down. I popped a shoulder and the tournament was over for me.'

When reaction to this has passed, the second judge says, 'Despite some flaws, let's say unavoidable flaws, I believe he was the wrestler of his generation. Only our host here had any consistent success against him.'

One judge against the Night Train, one judge for. Noble Dawn dabs at his forehead with the napkin before casting the deciding vote on his brother's character. The black eyes in his fat head find Chris. 'I visited his home recently and spoke to his mistress, the whore Tanaka. She told me she often feared for her life. Furthermore, she said he made her carry their bastard child.'

'Ah!'

The sashimi arrives on three great plates, cut in fine overlapping translucent strips and arranged as a rising spiral.

'I feel sorry for his younger brother,' continues Noble Dawn when the plates have been placed, 'because despite everything, the Night Train was like a father to him.'

All Chris can do is bow where he sits.

'He is where he belongs,' is the closing comment on the subject of his brother. Compliments fly on the artistry of the chef.

Driven by the sake, Chris stands and bows. 'Please forgive me. I came to deliver my brother's wish, in effect his dying wish, that his anger be forgiven by—'

'Enough,' snaps Noble Dawn. 'Come here.'

As Chris makes his way down the table, full of trepidation, Noble Dawn gestures to a waiter to bring him his jacket, from which he retrieves a white envelope. Casually, without making eye contact, he holds it out to Chris. 'For your family.'

'I can't accept that, sir.'

'Take it.'

'Sorry, but no. It's simply impossible.'

'Take it.'

To refuse twice is polite; to refuse the money a third time would be a gross insult. 'Thank you, but I have no family left to give it to, sir.'

'Get out, then!'

'Throw this dog out.'

Curses rise from the table and two men spring up, small men, who take hold of him roughly and escort him away.

Noble Dawn calls after him in his fat man's voice. 'I can't help you if you can't help yourself.'

Three waiters stand over him as he puts on his shoes in the reception area. The attendants are horror-stricken. Leaving, he expects a kick or at least a shove from the largest waiter following him. It doesn't happen. He's free on Empress Street, swept along with the crowd of Japanese diners and clubbers. He stops at a tiny hole-in-the-wall hamburger place, the type popular with drunks and teenagers. At one of the three barstools near the door, he angrily devours his Godzilla and chips and watches people stream by. Noble Dawn's attendant hurries past, or someone very much like him. As he finishes the burger, one of the waiters who ushered him out passes by in his black uniform, craning his head, looking intently up the street. His first guess is that they want to give him the money. How good would that make Noble Dawn look, he thinks: thanking his minions as they return to the table with the news that they have located little Ipswitch in a bar, who was very grateful and full of regret for his arrogance—a family trait. Either that, or they mean to do him physical harm. If so, they'll be armed. He sighs and wipes the grease from his fingers. How many more are looking for him? How many he's never seen before? He notices a taxi stand just up from the window, previously invisible to him. Kiwis only take taxis on their wedding day. In a moment he's reclining in the back seat, being borne away to safety.

At the guesthouse, in the quiet luxury of his room, his impulse to flee fades. He feels he has already got away, that perhaps his plan to leave Auckland immediately was a little rash, given that he's already paid for the night. Then again, Noble Dawn is a two-faced scumball who may well decide to have him murdered. Unsure whether to stay or leave, he leaves his key in the locked door and turns on the shower. As he waits in the bathroom for the steam to build before disrobing, he hears the door to his room rattle. He acts quickly: locks the bathroom door, and climbs out the large window into foliage. The shower continues to run, quieter, as his bare feet settle on damp earth. His car's right there; the keys, he knows, are in his pocket. In a flash he's across the cold concrete, into his car and away.

# Chapter 27:

# The hit

He gets lost several times in the tangle of roads leading out of the city, and his fury briefly transfers from Noble Dawn to the signage. When he eventually finds himself on the motorway heading south, he cries out, 'I'm coming, bro! Now we know who we're fighting!' He is ready to drive all night and make the early morning sailing from Wellington.

Three hours later, after the realisation that the morning ferry no longer runs, and the stress of being waved through a checkpoint, he stops by the side of the road. He's on the plateau north of Taupo. His bare feet are cold. The air pinches his ears and he breathes steam as he pisses. The pine forest has been recently logged. The land is stumped and ugly, ravaged, the timber on its way to Britain via Ireland, the money to Japan. The country is being bled dry. A wave of weariness comes over him and he knows he must sleep. But an hour after taking a motel room in Taupo and watching a Japanese baseball game on mute, he realises he won't be able to sleep and quietly leaves. For a while, back on the road, the thought of seeing his brother invigorates him. By the time he gets to Bulls he's flagging badly. His cries of 'I'm coming, bro!' won't clear away his exhaustion anymore. Just a couple of hours of sleep will do. Waiterere Beach strikes him as a good place to rest, if not in the bach with Hitomi, then in the car in a secluded place under pines.

When he pulls up in the driveway the bach is dark, as is number 3 over the road. There's no sign of anything amiss. He takes the gumboots outside the door, creeps over muddy grass down the side of the house and taps on the bedroom window. No reply. She must have left. He pushes the window and it slides up. Suddenly he's wide awake. Breaking in will not be conducive to sleep. He slides the window back down.

'Huh?'

'Hitomi?'

'Chris?'

'Yes.'

'Oh, one minute.'

She's looking for her wig, he thinks. Indeed, her wigged head soon appears at the window. She's wearing a T-shirt and knickers. She lifts the window hard and it bangs alarmingly.

'Oh,' she says. 'You can use the door if you like.'

'No, now I'm here.' As he heaves himself in, her hand taps impatiently on his back. A solemn kiss and then she hugs him hard. Pulling back, she says, 'I'm glad you came.'

'Me too.'


He's woken by the smell of a Kiwi breakfast under his nose. The boiled eggs and toast she's prepared are oddly touching. It's already late in the morning. He'll have to leave at around 8 pm for the late sailing to Lyttelton. She curls up and watches him eat. 'It's delicious,' he tells her, more than once.

When he's finished she says, 'It's cold today.'

He lights the fire and enjoys the process: splitting the logs out the back with the axe, splintering kindling with the hatchet, building a tepee frame over a ball of newspaper in

213

the grate, lighting it in four places, watching it take, building it up. He pulls up two armchairs and they warm their feet. Neither of them say much. They drink tea. An hour later Chris is woken by the cold to find Hitomi sleeping in her armchair beside him. He relights the fire.

They cook dinner together, a dish they call Kiwi-Japanese fusion: lightly fried balls of tinned tuna. He ends up eating all but one of them. Back in the glow of the fire, bracing himself to leave, he says, 'I found out who is behind my niece's murder.'

He waits for her to reply, but she just watches the fire. She's watching it so intently he decides she hasn't heard him. 'I found out who—'.

'Yes. Who is it?'

'An old opponent of my brother's, who holds a grudge for some reason.'

'What's his name?'

'Noble Dawn.'

'Oh, the great Noble Dawn. Huh.' She's flushed red.

'You know him?'

'Sorry, but he's famous for beating your brother. He's a living legend in Japan for that.'

'Why would he hate my brother?'

'I don't know. When it came to your older brother, people forgot sumo was sport, a show. People who never cared about sumo became passionately involved. For some people Noble Dawn's victories over the Night Train saved Japan's pride and honour.'

The fire burns.

'I've enjoyed hanging out with you today.' He smiles. 'Perhaps we should talk more?'

'Yes, but it takes time.' She nods emphatically. 'It should take time to find the right words.'

Chris watches the fire's steady combustion.

214

'I've been accused of getting my relationships back to front,' she adds. 'You're supposed to talk first—'

'And then go to bed.'

'Right.'

He feels that they're finding a new level of intimacy in front of the fire, talking and being silent. He thinks it might be a good time to confess he has visions of Johnny Lennon, and that the second vision saved him from death by hypothermia in a freezing river. He retrieves a couple of cassettes from his car. Back inside, he rewinds the first studio album, *Long Johnny Silver*, and opens the remaining bottle of wine. He finds he's anxious at what she will think as he pushes play.

'I've heard this before. Is he a Kiwi?'

He wants to say yes. 'He came from England as a little kid on a Compassion ship during the famine of '46, when the Russians were expected to invade. Occupied New Zealand was seen as a better bet by some. There was food.'

'Oh.'

'Actually, his mother didn't want him to come. His father secretly took him to the dock, intending to sneak away. But Johnny's mother and her boyfriend turned up just before they were about to leave. There was this big argument by the ship and Johnny's father forced him to choose. He was five. Can you imagine that? And he chose his mother twice, but as his father walked up the gangplank he started to cry and followed him.'

'Poor kid.'

'Yeah.'

'Are these his songs?'

He'd like to say they are. 'No, it's mainly covers on this album, covers of songs by American musicians. Chuck Berry, Bob Dylan. This one's a Paul McCartney song though.'

'Is he a Kiwi?'

'No, he's English, from the same town as Lennon, funnily enough. McCartney actually covered one of his songs a few years back, which is pretty major.'

His desire to tell her about his visions retreats as side one plays itself out ineffectually in the oddly formal setting with its red wine, real fire, and this older woman listening conscientiously. The lyrics on the rock 'n' roll tracks seem mundane, embarrassing. It occurs to him that the visions of Lennon came only when he was extremely stressed or wasted. The first visitation, in the cell in Christchurch, came after he hadn't slept for twenty-four hours, when he feared for his life. There was still a lot of hashish in his system the second time. Lennon was clearly a product of his subconscious.

'I like his later stuff better,' he says. It feels like a betrayal.

'Put it on.'

'Not right now,' he says tersely and pours himself another wine.

The phone rings. Hitomi holds her fingers to her lips and takes the call in the bedroom.

'The owner,' she says when she returns. 'Can I have a glass of wine?'

'I thought you were allergic?'

'I am. I can have one.'

She seems nervous about drinking it though. Not long after the first sip, her face is pink.

'Are you okay?'

'Yes.'

'What happens if you have two glasses?'

'My face swells up. Ha. And gets very red. My eyes too.'

She finishes the glass somewhat heroically in his eyes. It takes a toll. He's touched by her willingness to share a moment with him. He doesn't want to leave to catch the ferry. He wants to spend one more night with her before the trials that wait in Christchurch.

'I'll be in the bathroom,' she says apologetically.

The fire crackles and the cassette hums, having run to the end but not stopped automatically. A distinctive resonant nasal voice fills the room. 'I was a violent young man and I died violently.'

Chris jumps up. It's a cassette, not a record, so there can be no hidden message in the run-out. He pushes the stop button.

'That's why I went on about peace and love so much in my last years,' Lennon's voice says from the speakers. Chris ejects the cassette, his heart thumping. *Am I mad?*

Silence returns, the pop and crackle of fire. He stares at the cassette in his hand.

'But I came around to a new way of thinking shortly before I was murdered. I felt that peace should not be bought at *any* price. *That's* the reason I was murdered, actually.'

'Where are you?' Chris whispers.

'It's very dark and cramped. Suffocating.'

'What can you see?'

'Fire.'

'Can you move?'

'No.'

*This*, Chris thinks, *is God's justice?*

'Hang on.'

The front of the left speaker is kicked out by a foot in a white sneaker. Somehow Lennon, full-size, clad in an off-white suit and sporting his late-era Buddy Holly glasses and gingery sideburns, climbs out of it. He stretches luxuriously. 'Ah, that's better.' Eyeing the broken speaker he says, 'I always was a fan of mono.' He turns and stands with his back to the warming fire, looks at the ceiling thoughtfully. His large sideburns cast a pale copper glow on his white suit, in the way a buttercup glows a chin yellow. Looking down,

Lennon fixes Chris gravely in the eye. 'Of all the martial arts, Chris, I favour Aikido. But sometimes in self-defence you have to hurt your attacker, even stop him for good, you know. Sometimes it's you and your family or him.' Opening his palms and drawing a deep breath, Lennon is about to speak again when the sound of the bathroom door opening disappears him, and repairs the speaker.

'I need to lie down,' Hitomi says.

'I'll join you.'

She shakes him awake. 'Chris, Chris.' Tears are running down her face. She's been crying for a while.

'What?'

'They're coming to kill you.'

'Who are?'

'Noble Dawn's men.' She slips back and hunches in the space between the wall and bed in anticipation of a beating.

'I won't hurt you. Tell me.'

'They're coming to kill you. You must leave.'

'When?'

'Soon. At 3 o'clock.'

It's 2:15. 'Have they spoken to you?'

She nods. 'You must go.'

'Will Noble Dawn come?'

'I don't know.'

He sits up and she flinches. 'I won't hurt you,' he says. It takes fifteen minutes to untangle her, for her to believe he won't hit her.

Then she holds him. 'I love you. Really, I think I always have. I'm crazy, you know.'

'We're okay, Hitomi. It's the world that's crazy.'

'Huh.' A smile flashes across her face.

'We can run, or kill Noble Dawn and run.'

'Where can we go?'

'There's a place.'

'Where?'

'The Ureweras, on the east coast. We can leave tonight and join the resistance.'

'Oh.'

'They'll embrace you, I'm sure.'

'As a hostage?'

'No, Hitomi, as a fighter, as a source of information, as a symbol of the struggle.'

'What else can we do? Right? I'll try.'


She is supposed to leave the front door open if he is asleep, and wait in the bathroom from 3 am. They wait together in the lounge, which is very dark even with the door open, and peek between a gap in the curtains. At 3 precisely a large black sedan pulls up. The brakes flare red then go out. He squeezes her hand, and she goes to the door. A man gets out of the car: Noble Dawn's attendant.

'I did the job myself,' Hitomi announces as she walks towards the car.

Another man in a suit gets out. A man he hasn't seen before.

'Poison,' she says jauntily.

'Really?'

'And a plastic bag to be sure.'

'Oh.' The men look at each other. 'Well.'

'Come and see,' she trills.

They follow her. The second doesn't bother to draw his gun. She waits for the second man and stops him to say something he finds amusing. He's several metres behind the first as Chris takes up his position inside the door with the hatchet raised above his head. He's practised the blow several times, so it will be automatic when the time comes.

His resolve has been steeled by Lennon's last visit. The time for talking and apologising, he tells himself as the footsteps approach, is over. The attendant walks in and drops under a clean strike; he's out for good before he even hits the floor. The pistol in his hand presents an opportunity, but there's no time to change the plan, only enough to pull the body a couple of metres to the side.

'I would like that very much,' Hitomi is saying to the second man as he reaches the door.

'Good,' he replies, and stops.

It's too dark for him to see anything immediately. Instinct makes him pause. Chris holds his breath, the hatchet over his head. The silencer on the end of the man's pistol comes into view. *Should I grab it?*

'Uh.' The man lurches forward, pushed by Hitomi. The first blow strikes the shoulder of his gun hand; the second blow drops him. The third is probably unnecessary.

'Wave and shut the door,' Chris says as he takes up the pistols. His hands are shaking, he's panting.

'They expected to have me after killing you,' she says bitterly.

*'Can you use a gun?'*

'Yes.'

'Go out to the car with the pistol behind you, like this.' He puts it in the back of her jeans. 'Shoot the driver. If Noble Dawn's there, leave him to me.'

She practises drawing the gun out a couple of times.

'Good luck.'

She steps outside, waves cheerfully to the car and walks down the driveway, the pistol's silencer in her waistband. She is acting much cooler than Chris feels. The driver rolls his window down. He can't tell if anyone's behind him.

'Do you want a cup of tea?' she calls.

'Tea?'

'Yes, or something a little stronger?' At the car window now, her hand creeps around for the gun. She steps back, plants her feet, points with a two-hand grip, and fires. Chris is at the car in a second, wrenching open the rear door. Noble Dawn's face is speckled with blood. Impassive, he stares straight ahead.

'Get out,' Chris tells him.

'No,' Hitomi says, 'he's too big to move.'

Chris trains his pistol on Noble Dawn's temple. It's trembling in his hand. *Do I just shoot him?* Noble Dawn continues to stare out the front window, as if nothing has happened, as if his driver's blood isn't sprayed across his face. He blinks slowly.

'I suppose you want to know why,' Noble Dawn says glumly, still looking straight ahead.

'Yes.'

'Can I have a cigarette?'

'Don't move, I'll give you one. Hitomi, light one for him.' He cautiously hands over the lit cigarette.

Noble Dawn takes a big drag. *'Menthol?'* He flashes a glance at Chris for the first time.

'Take it or leave it.'

He takes another drag and smoke jets from his nostrils. 'Recently your big brother found himself isolated. It hurt his pride. He started drinking too much and telling people he threw the bouts I won against him in Japan.' Noble Dawn blinks heavily and taps ash onto the knee of his suit pants. 'I should have been celebrated after my years in the ring, not snickered at behind my back in restaurants.'

Chris's finger tightens on the trigger. He nearly pulls it. 'You lie. My brother would never throw a fight.'

'Many of us threw one occasionally to help a colleague keep his ranking. Some even threw bouts for money. Your older brother did it to get out of Japan alive in '79 and '80.'

Chris feels that Noble Dawn's calm is a way of jeering at him and his shaking pistol. 'He couldn't win *everything*, Little Train. We are a proud people. But here is the thing. These agreements between wrestlers are always kept secret. To the grave. Always.'

'Your retirement's been ruined?'

'Rumours began to reach Japan. They had to stop.'

'So to punish him you murdered Sarah and Chiyo?'

Still staring ahead, Noble Dawn flicks the half-finished menthol cigarette into the front seat. He rolls his shoulders once.

'I mean Patrick's little girl, Sarah,' Chris says, 'and his wife Chiyo, the *whore Tanaka*, as you called her.'

'*Wife?*'

The pistol sneezes. The corpse retains its sitting position; the head hangs, pillowed on chin and neck.

Chris stands and looks over the roof of the car to the pines. A roaring noise fills his ears. The house over the road is in darkness. Suddenly weak at the knees, he sits on the pavement.

'It's this easy?' Hitomi says.

'Huh?'

'What shall we do now?'

His thoughts are washed away as if by a torrent of water. She stares at him, waiting for instruction, as he slowly stands. He walks to the ragged apple tree and picks up the figurine of his brother. The cool white porcelain smears red. It's someone else's blood. He stares at its happy little face.

# Epilogue

A sharp crack and a shiver of leaves; a louder crack and the car is gone, hidden in dense bush. They stand in gloom on the gravel road above the gully, in their tourist-new green bush-shirts and packs, with the pistols fastened to them with bungy cords. The car's sudden and emphatic disappearance, the approaching night, and the silence and smells of the Urewera bush send deep currents of anxiety through him. He plays their new torch over the foliage below. Its beam is feeble.

'Gone,' says Hitomi, peering down from the edge of the road. She wears a black beanie over her blond wig. Her mouth forms a rueful expression.

It feels to Chris that they are being listened to, as if the bush itself is hostile, hosting the gathering of spirits as light leaves the sky. A memory of the lifeless assassins on the bach floor, of the struggle with Noble Dawn's corpse to get it prone in the back seat and out of sight, makes him take her hand. His own death may come as easily as theirs, but she is likely to suffer the horrors unique to women captured in war. *It must not happen to her.*

Now they must walk all night into the unknown and not fall into a trap, get stuck on some bluff, or blunder around in circles. The approaching dark and her hand's tender warmth shoulder him a vast responsibility. He knows the hardest test is yet to come.